There was a whisper of stee
Rand felt a flash of fire along
a pace back along the corri............ ....g.. ....gger of
the Linebaugh, knowing that if he squeezed it he was likely to
break his own wrist.

"Joe, out here!" the man yelled, grinning wolfishly. The knife
darted again, and Dave retreated once more. Warm blood
trickled down his arm and over the fingers of his left hand.

The dancing steel kept him going backward, level with the
empty doorway of Room Five. Then a second man appeared
in the passage, holding a machine pistol in his hands. Dave
leapt sideways into the room. The moment he was out of sight,
he dropped into a shooter's crouch, bracing his right wrist with
his bloodied left hand. He waited.

"What's he got?" came a high-pitched voice.

"Big Magnum. But he hasn't used it. Means the skinny bastard won't."

The speaker immediately jumped into the doorway, a thin
murderous smile pasted on to the unshaven cheeks.

"Wrong," Dave said, feeling the smooth action of the trigger
and the familiar brutal kick that jarred clear to the shoulder.

James McPhee

SURVIVAL 2000
RENEGADE WAR

A GOLD EAGLE BOOK FROM
WORLDWIDE.

TORONTO • NEW YORK • LONDON • PARIS
AMSTERDAM • STOCKHOLM • HAMBURG
ATHENS • MILAN • TOKYO • SYDNEY

This one is for George Wright and for
Michael, who finally persuaded me to
discard my chisel and tablet of stone and
crawl into the techno-century. With
thanks for all of their help over
many years.

First edition June 1991

ISBN 0-373-63202-9

RENEGADE WAR

Snow had fallen, snow on snow, snow on snow,
In the deep mid-winter, long, long ago.
—Christina Rossetti
1830–1894

1

David Rand stared through the grimy window. Outside, the world was fast in the desolate grip of a deep winter—a new ice age not even remotely like the nuclear winter people had feared in the last few decades of the twentieth century.

When disaster struck in 2049, it had not been created by human hands. It was ironic, David thought, that after all the talk of mankind over-reaching itself, probing the mysteries of life and matter, splitting atoms and genes with equal ease, the whole issue had been swept aside by a deadly manifestation of the awesome power of nature.

The dark visitation had come from space... tiptoeing in softly amid the reassurances of governments everywhere that there was nothing to be feared. Finally it nearly tore the Earth from its moorings in space.

When the asteroid Adastreia—aptly named the Inescapable—streaked through the atmosphere, it broke into several large chunks. The largest impacted near Roanoke, Virginia. Other sections hit various parts of the globe—near Beijing, Munich, the Amazon—but always with devastating effect.

Each asteroid strike threw a monstrous cloud of liquefied earth and dust far above Earth's atmosphere, and the dense layer of matter absorbed the planet's heat and reflected back into space the incoming warmth of the sun.

The world became a deep-freeze, torn apart by violent earthquakes and volcanoes, with tidal waves more than a mile high crashing against the shores. Jets of molten lava spurted out for more than a hundred miles in all directions, and the Earth's magnetic field was radically altered.

And David Rand, who had been living the American dream of success and contentment, had seen an unimaginable collapse. Along the East Coast, the major urban centers—New York, Boston, Washington—were destroyed, and Chicago and the low-lying lands flanking the Mississippi were ravaged beyond description. The San Andreas and Hayward faults became like giants awakened; most of western California vanished beneath the tumbling waves of the Pacific Ocean.

Governments ceased to exist, and the people who survived the immediate terrors died in huge numbers from thirst, hunger and pestilence.... Only mass graves could accommodate the dead. Reason and sanity, always in shorter supply than needed, completely left the world.

And among the scattered pockets of survivors were the mad, the ruthless, the malevolent, driven to preying on the weaker ones who had managed to retain their humanity. The dark, primeval forces in men's souls took over, roaming the ruins like pre-historic monsters.

Turning from the window, David looked down at the wobbly green eyes of the rag doll in his hand. Mr. Boffo, Roxanne had called it, and she always had to have the cuddly toy in her bed at night to chase away the monsters....

But now his daughters, Ellie and Roxanne, were the captives of a renegade band of army deserters, and his wife, Janine, lay dead in the grounds just outside the window. He had survived, along with Lee, his young son, who was being thrust into an early and violent manhood.

It was as though their lives had been wrenched back to the depth of the Dark Ages, and the way things had been before seemed like something only dreamed....

DAVID ALEXANDER RAND, age thirty-five, had been an accountant in Bakersfield, California, where he owned a beautiful home perched high in the Sierras, on Highridge Canyon Road in Cody

Heights, not far from Bakersfield. He had been a keen survivalist and a member of the local shooting club, but never dreamed that one day his very existence would depend on such skills.

A few days before the impact of Adastreia, not believing, along with everybody else, that there was any serious danger, Dave and his sixteen-year-old son, Lee, were camping in the Cibola National Forest, fifty miles west of Socorro, New Mexico. With them was their brindled pit bull, called Melmoth. His wife, Janine Rand, had taken their two daughters on a visit to Memphis—Ellie, nearly fifteen, and Roxanne, eight.

Dave and Lee were unharmed by the initial effects of the Big Hit, and ended up staying where they were, living off the land. They fully believed that Janine and the girls had been killed.

After witnessing some scenes of murderous violence, they finally decided to try to return to their home in California. On August 17, 2050, they reached the house to find it undamaged. There was a card in their mailbox, posted by Janine two days before the strike, telling them that she had taken Ellie and Roxanne to stay with her mother— Granny Bronsky—in Montana.

Dumbstruck by the news but still afraid to believe that the rest of their family would be found alive, Dave and his son immediately agreed they must try and get up there, despite the dangers of the journey. So they loaded up their Trackbreaker four-by and set off through the wintry landscape toward Montana.

On the way they met a young woman called Zera, and she accompanied them on their dangerous journey northward through increasingly hostile country.

When they finally reached their destination, tragedy lay in wait for them.

A gang of murderous thugs, mostly army deserters, had been holding sway over the area under the leadership of a blond giant named Sheever. After looting and raping in the small township in Montana, the group headed off on horseback toward the east and their secret hideout. But Dave managed to get an idea where they were headed, and he became determined to pursue them.

His motive was simple. Not only had Sheever taken Janine's life, but he had also kidnapped both Ellie and Roxanne. David found it impossible to bring himself to think of the fate of the two girls. The only thing he was capable of doing was to make the blind attempt to get them back—or die trying....

2

For a long time David Rand sat in the cold room, holding Mr. Boffo. He remembered that the rag doll had been Granny Bronsky's gift on Roxanne's third birthday. Every few months Janine had performed major surgery on it, sewing up cuts and tears, patching and mending.

Now Granny Bronsky was eighteen months dead, buried in the trim cemetery at the top of the hill on the eastern approach to the town. She had died of heart failure within a few days of the Big Hit.

Janine Rand had died less than a week before. Dave knew he would reproach himself for the rest of his life for not having made better time on their drive north to Montana. Four days sooner and he might have been able to save Janine's life.

He stood and again looked out of the cracked window, over the blown snow to where there had once been a garden swing on a trim lawn. Now there was piled earth, frosted over, and a rudimentary marker made from an old cupboard door. Dave wasn't close enough to see the black writing, but he knew it by heart and would carry the words to his own grave: "Janine Rand, daughter, wife and mother. Murdered here September 2050. Pray for her."

What was it Harry Wexell, the old man who was once the county sheriff, had said? Something that he'd wanted to add to the marker but there wasn't enough room.

Then Dave remembered. "May she run forever beneath God's good sun." The echo of his own voice in the wrecked room brought him back from the wintry desolation outside.

There was a deal to be done before they could set off in pursuit of the man called Sheever and his gang. Wexell had led Dave to the dying Hogan, left behind by Sheever's men, and Dave had forcibly made him tell where his gang's hideout was—in a box canyon, above an exclusive ski resort about 150 miles to the east.

That had been the previous day. Dave wondered whether anyone would bother to dispose of Hogan's corpse, or whether it would be left to rot like so many millions of other bodies.

Locally, there had been a virulent epidemic of cholera, which had been responsible for Sheever's finally leading the surviving members of his gang away. They had terrorized the district for far too long.

Dave was startled when Lee came into the bedroom and stood in the doorway. "Hey. You found Mr. Boffo, Dad."

"Yeah. I don't know how Roxie could have left it behind when she moved out."

"Likely had no choice."

Dave looked at his son, his eyes cold as Sierra meltwater. "That's probably right."

"When do we move?"

"Soon as we're ready. Harry reckons we could be in for some double-shit weather."

"We're low on gas."

Dave sighed. "I know. And Sheever didn't leave any around here. Used it on snow buggies."

"If they went out on horses, then it must mean that they'd run out of gas, too."

"Best check on the Trackbreaker. The only plan I can come up with is to go after them as far and fast as possible, once we've got all the provisions we can. Should be ready to go by first light tomorrow. Have you fed Melmoth?"

The teenager shook his head. "No. Zera's looked after him since last night." He turned to go out again, then hesitated in the hall. "Dad?"

"What is it, Lee?"

"Zera."

"What about her?"

"Now Mom's . . . you know, dead, so does that mean that you and her are going to . . . ?"

"Doesn't change things. She still intending to come with us?"

"Says so."

"She can drive and shoot some. Three of us have just a bit better chance than two of us."

Lee persisted. "But you and her. I know that you . . . that night. I heard you." Hastily he added, "I wasn't spying or anything like that, Dad."

"I'm sure you weren't." He hadn't realized that his lovemaking with the girl had been overheard by his son. "It was once. She was . . . I was lonely and . . . Didn't mean anything, though."

The boy grinned. "That's keying fine, Dad. I wasn't sort of skedding off about you. Just that . . . I like her a lot and—" He drew a deep breath. "Whatever you do is okay with me, Dad."

"All right. Thanks for the vote of confidence, Lee. Look, I've been thinking. Weather's closing in and likely to get worse. I reckon we'd do better now to ditch the trailer."

"It's three-quarters empty. Even if we can scrounge some more food, there'll still be room inside the truck."

"Just what I was thinking. That's one of the things to do today. Discard anything that's not vital. I want to travel light and fast."

HARRY WEXELL CAME trudging up the hill with a quarter-carcass of a deer on a small-wheeled cart towed behind him. He also brought a couple of tins of soup. The labels had peeled off them. "But I'm sure they're soup," he said, handing the cans to David. "Everything else in the same box was soup."

The old man helped them unload the trailer. Dave told him to help himself to anything he could find a use for.

In the afternoon, while Wexell went over the road map with Lee and Zera, Dave decided to pay a visit to his wife's grave.

The sun had broken through, casting a watery, golden light over the trampled lawn. As he walked past what had once been Granny Bronsky's small pool of carp, he found a pile of ejected cartridge cases. He stooped and picked one up, holding the dull brass in the palm of his hand.

He guessed that it was 5.56 caliber, probably from an automatic assault rifle. That lent credence to something Harry had said about Sheever's gang operating with some signs of military discipline, as though they were army deserters. If they had a good array of sophisticated automatic weapons, rescuing Ellie and Roxanne was going to be tough.

He paused as he reached the marker on the pile of shoveled earth, and looked around at some of the most beautiful scenery on God's earth. The high mountains to the north off toward Canada were like pictures drawn by a talented child. Sharp-peaked, covered in snow, with dark ravines sliced into their flanks. Clouds were gathered about some of the tops, and Dave could just catch the faint sound of distant thunder. Since the asteroid hit, the weather had been dramatically erratic, with storms of unearthly violence swooping in with little or no warning.

This afternoon there was only a lightish breeze from the west, rustling the dried leaves on the ground about his feet. Somewhere beyond the edges of the spread there was the noise of a river. On previous visits Dave had walked down there with Janine to sit on the bank, each content in the company of the other. That content had been diminishing over the past couple of years in ways that Dave had never been able to quite understand.

From the volume of sound, he guessed that the water was in full spate. From behind him came a sudden burst of laughter. Zera's voice. He eased the big Linebaugh pistol on his hip and turned back to the grave.

For a few moments he closed his eyes, self-consciously wondering if the tears were going to flow.

Nothing happened. His nose tickled, and he had the urge to sneeze. Standing there, Dave felt foolish, wondering what had possessed him to enact this scene. He'd seen so many vids with the grieving husband stooped over his wife's grave, talking to the dear departed. Telling her how things were with the family and asking advice about an errant child.

"Jan... I'm sorry, but I can't think of anything to say," he said, embarrassed at how loud his voice seemed to be. "I was going to, like, tell you we're going after the girls, and... well, I'll give my own life if I have to, just to get them back." In his heart he didn't feel the conviction, the way he had earlier. It was due to the fact, he realized, that some part of him was standing apart in the role of spectator.

From the other side of the house, he heard the roar of the Trackbreaker's engine starting up, followed by clouds of blue-gray smoke drifting above the roof. Harry and Lee were servicing the vehicle.

He looked down again at the grave. "I'll never forget you, Jan. I know times weren't so good as they once were.... But, Christ, I didn't want this!"

HARRY HAD ALSO BROUGHT the best part of a bottle of bourbon on his rickety cart. "Sorry, it was brewed in Japan," he said.

It was the first alcohol Dave had seen in a long while, and he savored the burn at the back of his throat. Lee only sipped at it, but Zera offered her chipped mug for a refill.

"Tastes good, Harry," she said, beaming at him. Her bright blue eyes glinted in the reflected light of the setting sun. Her hair was long enough now to need tying with a length of black ribbon.

The weather was still reasonably good, almost like an ordinary, old-fashioned fall afternoon. Some of the trees that had survived the Strike were donning their robes of fiery gold and crimson and the air smelled clean and fresh.

"Like old times, Dave," Harry said. "Sitting with friends as the day sinks away, getting on a real good glow."

"I'll drink to that. You sure you don't want to come with us, Harry?"

Wexell sniffed. "I appreciate the offer, Dave, and I'd surely like to see those bastards burned off. But

I'm old, and Doc Murtry told me three years ago I should start taking it easy. I'd be in the way.''

"Yeah, you would," said Zera, draining her drink, then looking at the bottle in Harry's gnarled fingers and showing her disappointment that it was empty.

"Zera!" Dave felt his anger swell at her callous remark.

"What?"

"You don't fucking talk like that to—"

But the old lawman shook his head, interrupting him. "You're getting past it, Dave. Last of the lost generation. Girlie's got the ace on the line. 'Course I'd be in the damned way. And if you don't have the balls to up and say that, Dave, then you're going to be as much use as a lead tomato to those little ones of your'n."

Zera stood up and kissed him on the top of his weathered, balding head. "That's right, Harry. Nothing personal."

"Hell, I know that," he said with a grin.

SHE CAME TO HIM in the night again, slipping inside the big sleeping bag, waking him. Her arms around him were tight, and she rubbed her body provocatively against his. "It'll be fine, Dave," she whispered. "We'll find them and they'll be fine."

He didn't answer her then, as he became lost in her warm curves, burying his face in her hair. There was no more talk, just their hot breaths mingling and their limbs locked in the heated give-and-take.

Later, when she had fallen asleep snuggled into his arms, Dave thought about what she had said and wondered why women liked to soothe their men. It was easier, for sure, to have blind faith. But he had been a witness to many unspeakable acts and circumstances, and he didn't know from where she drew such smug reassurance. It was the eternal instinct, he supposed, to delay facing reality and to postpone anxiety... and to placate men. Not that he needed placating, because he was not unreasonable. He allowed himself a sigh as he stared into the night, not able to imagine a future, not being really able to look anywhere off in time except the past, the only solid landmark.

Just before he drifted off, he allowed himself a wry smile when he remembered the worries people had before the Hit—making enough money; quarreling with their wives, children, girlfriends, husbands; inequality between the sexes; fulfilling their lives and amounting to something.... All that had become dust and ashes. Now they were looking for their next meager meal most of the time, and blindly trying to stay alive—and nobody was sure why....

ABOUT A HUNDRED MILES away, the fire at the center of the camp was blazing brightly. Around the perimeter, armed men were patrolling a regular beat. Though there was little chance of anyone being such a terminal fool as to attack his well-prepared force, Sheever wasn't taking chances.

He sat near the fire, nobody close to him, smoking a thin cigar. The light from the crackling logs was so intense it made his blond hair look white as fresh-fallen snow.

Most of his men were asleep, wrapped in blankets. One of the tethered horses snorted as its sensitive nostrils caught the faint scent of a prowling bear.

Among the trees, with an armed man watching them, the females slept. Four of them. One in her thirties, restless, aware even in sleep that Sheever might summon her at any moment. Another woman, younger, lying flat on her back, hands at her sides. They'd insisted on her sleeping that way in the convent, and old practices die hard.

Sharing a sleeping bag were two girls. One of them was in her teens, the other nearer to nine. Roxanne had cried herself to rest, with Ellie's arms locked about her.

3

It was a bleak dawn as Dave Rand shook hands with Harry Wexell.

"Thanks for everything."

"You're welcome, son."

"Keep an eye on Jan's grave for me. Maybe put a bunch of flowers on it, come the spring."

Wexell nodded. "Good as done, Dave. Take care on the road."

"We will."

"And don't take no chances with that big bitching bastard Sheever. Get him in the cross hairs and squeeze the trigger. Don't hesitate."

"Not a second's thought for that, Harry."

Dave climbed into the driving seat of the dark green Trackbreaker, slammed the door shut and used the manual handle to wind down the window. Lee was strapped in the front passenger seat, his eyes staring blankly ahead. Zera was huddled in the back, with Melmoth lying at her side.

The engine coughed into life. During the previous day Lee and Zera had worked together, trying to service the four-by. The main problem was that the vehicle had been driven over terrain much worse than anything it had been designed for. And the miles had taken their toll. It had already lost one tire to a blowout, and Dave guessed that the spare wasn't going to last them very much longer. The transmission had become sticky, and the tracking had been damaged by impact with a massive boulder somewhere in north Idaho.

"So long!" shouted Harry Wexell, waving a hand to them.

The Trackbreaker moved away, its wheels kicking up a shower of gravel and ice chips. There was a moment in the curve of the drive when a sideways glance would have given Dave a last glimpse of Janine's grave, but he kept his eyes ahead.

After the relatively mild weather of the past day or so, the skies were closing in once more. Within the first hour of the journey there was a savage hailstorm, with chunks of ice as large as billiard balls pounding on the roof of the truck.

Melmoth didn't like the noise and began to whine, flattening himself on the upholstery. Zera started to gentle him, whispering and rubbing her hand along the taut sinews under the pit bull's chin.

"Road we came on...it'll be completely undrivable if the snows come hard," Lee voiced his thoughts.

"Could be. That's why we have to make the best time we can—until the tire goes or we run out of gas or run out of highway."

Zera piped up from the back seat. "Then what, Dave? Huh?"

"Then we find some other way of moving on. Worst comes to worst, we walk."

The young woman laughed, sounding genuinely amused. "I can't wait."

FROM THE MAP, it was obvious that on horseback Sheever and his gang had a great advantage. On an open road the four-by would have done fifty miles to their ten. But the motor vehicle was powerless to follow them across mountain trails. That meant detours, long and expensive detours.

By the end of two days of limited progress, Dave Rand was beginning to lose heart.

His first and best plan had been to retrace his own steps, until he reached the place where he'd hidden and watched Sheever and his party ride by. But the warmer weather had melted some of the higher snow, which had surged into the rivers, causing flash floods to wash out the trails.

On the second night they camped in the lee of an overhang of rock, snug against the cold drizzle that had begun to fall around sundown. While Lee got the stove going, Dave and Zera checked the tires of their transport.

"Won't last much longer," she said. "Then we dump it?"

"No. Then we drive on as far as we can on three wheels. *Then* we dump it."

"I hate this shitty weather. I wish it'd either get warmer or colder. Wetter or drier. Can't stand this endless soft rain."

Dave straightened, wiping mud off the knees of his jeans. "It's a bastard for getting a fire going. Not a splinter of dry wood for fifty miles around. The gas cylinders won't last us forever."

"What if Sheever sees the smoke?"

"Not much smoke from one little cooking stove, Zera. More of a problem if there's anyone near that smells the stew heating."

They walked back to camp together through the dank, dripping forest. For the fiftieth time, it crossed Dave's mind that he should come out and talk about their relationship. But he feared she would look at him, raising her eyebrows with mock puzzlement, and ask him what relationship he was talking about. So, for the fiftieth time, he kept silent.

Melmoth had recovered from the scare of the hailstorm and came bounding eagerly toward them, his stumpy tail wagging enthusiastically. Suddenly he checked and turned to the side, muzzle sniffing in the direction of the depths of the woods.

"What is it, boy? What've you seen? Or heard?"

"Or scented?" offered Zera.

The dog was walking stiff-legged toward a narrow path that edged between a lightning-blasted larch and a stunted live oak. Dave and Zera followed him. The Linebaugh was cocked and ready in the man's right hand, while the woman held her plated .32-caliber Ruger.

Lee had heard his father call out and came running from the overhang, carrying his Onyx scattergun. "What's up, Dad?"

"Melmoth. There's nothing we can see, but he just went off at a tangent."

The dog had stopped, all the short hairs along his spine bristling.

They followed, pausing just behind him. Lee laughed. "It's just a big pile of shit!"

Zera shook her head. "It's not *just* a pile of shit, Lee. Look, there in that patch of wet mud to the side of it."

Dave grabbed Melmoth by the collar and pulled him back. "All right, boy. All right." He peered where Zera had pointed. "Yeah. You're right, Zera. Bear track. Big one. It'll be crowded, but we'll all sleep in the truck tonight.'' They'd been taking turns sleeping out in the open since they'd left the house in Montana, but the prospect of being jerked away by half a ton of hungry grizzly wasn't too attractive.

But three of them sleeping in the Trackbreaker turned out not to be the best fun in the world, either. Dave and Lee slept more or less upright without reclining the front seats, while Zera stretched out in the back.

They agreed that in future they would take turns with the luxury of the long rear seat.

As they pushed through the frozen countryside the next day, Dave would stop the vehicle every now and again to get out and walk, looking on the ground for signs that they were still on the trail of Sheever and his party.

Despite the occasional falls of fresh snow, he found enough evidence to convince him that the dying Hogan had told him the truth about the gang's destination. There were many piles of horse droppings, as well as heaps of cans and broken bottles surrounding the circles of gray ash where camp fires had been.

And, a day later, they came across an unburied corpse.

"Shit!"

The Trackbreaker slewed hard to the left as Lee tugged at the steering wheel. Dave was dozing in the back, and he snapped awake from a dream in which he and Janine had been pursuing one of their children along the empty corridors of a gigantic office block. It was filled with an overbright, singing sense of empty space, but the windows were all mirrors, making it impossible to see out. The strange part of the dream was that David and his dead wife were not hunting for Lee or Ellie or Roxanne, but for the son she'd had, between the girls. Stillborn, the umbilical cord wound taut about the soft neck.

As he sat up and rubbed his eyes, the dream began to retreat from him. "What . . . ?"

"Looks like a body, Dad."

There was a veil of ice and packed snow over the grille, and Dave cautiously opened the door, whistling at the cold. A heaven of sunset was swelling over to the west, above the surrounding hills.

He saw the corpse immediately.

All he could tell at first glance was that it was probably male, though the birds of prey had done a good job on the soft tissues of face and naked body. It lay propped against the bole of a medium-sized redwood, the head tilted stiffly to the left, the eye sockets empty, staring blindly at the sky. The flesh was torn and pale, but there was very little blood, showing that the man had been dead before he was dumped there.

Lee started to get out after his father, but Dave spun around and shouted to him, "No! Keep the engine running. Nothing to be done here."

Zera rolled the window down on the passenger side and called out, her breath frosting the air in front of her face. "What did he die of?"

There wasn't any wound that Dave could see, and the emaciated state of the corpse made him suspect the cause of death was probably cholera. Since there was another of the litter-strewn campsites nearby, it was obvious that it had been one of Sheever's men.

"Still on the right track," Dave said, as he climbed back into the warmth of the four-by, slamming the door hard behind him.

The next morning a sharp turn in the narrow highway brought them to the brink of a scenic overlook. Dave remembered that Janine had always called a view like this a *vista encantadora.* And this one was truly enchanting.

He was at the wheel and he eased down to a halt, pulling on the hand brake and conscious of how little play remained in it. Looking around, he turned off the engine.

"Why've we stopped?" asked Lee.

"Got to piss."

"Me, too," said Zera, opening her door and jumping out. "God, what a double-lovely view. Look at the light on those cliffs on the far side of the valley. Wish I had my sketchbook."

Dave joined her. "You draw?"

"Some. Took classes at college. Not very good, though." She laughed nervously. "Isn't it kind of strange, Dave?"

"What?"

"The way we have normal conversations in this abnormal world. How are you? What do you do for a living? Where do you live? Did you like the last Lori Kirton flick? Have you eaten Japanese? God, it's so weird!"

Now Lee also joined them, Melmoth at his side. "It's beautiful. I really think the weather is getting better, Dad."

"Maybe. Got to go and have a piss before I burst. Don't go far from the truck and keep an eye on the dog, Lee."

"Sure."

Standing in the fringe of the forest, Dave could look out beyond the trees, past the bare edge of dried earth, frost-rippled, toward the great cleft of the river valley and the mountains. The air smelled like heaven, fresh and clean. He unzipped his jeans and started to urinate, the amber stream pattering on the rotted pine needles. It steamed in the cool air.

He smiled to himself at the odd feeling of guilt he was experiencing. He half expected the heavy hand of a serious-faced park ranger on his shoulder. "We would prefer it if you used the available facilities, sir. The delicate balance of the ecosystem is easily disturbed by antisocial behavior like this." The imaginary scene made him feel like a six-year-old caught by a solemn and incredibly wise uncle.

Dave finished and zipped himself up again, then moved a few paces away, out into the scarce sunlight, shading his eyes.

He saw something across the valley, in the direction they were heading. Probably twenty miles away by winding trails, but barely a direct mile from where he stood. In the unmoving panorama, with no other sign of life in evidence, a thin column of pale smoke curled lazily into the sky.

"Lee!" he shouted. "Zera! Come on. Let's get moving!"

They piled into the vehicle, eager to catch up to their quarry. Before they could close in on where they'd seen the smoke, they had to descend the near side of the valley. The highway was in good condition, showing little evidence of damage from quakes, but it was very steep and narrow. Dave had let his son take the wheel and sat in the passenger seat, hanging on the strap, trying to balance against the pitching and rolling on the hairpin bends.

"Easy, boy, easy," he muttered.

"Relax, Dad."

Miraculously they reached the bottom without bursting through the rusted guard fence into the deeps beneath. The road flattened, going over a trim bridge, then along a straight stretch before starting to climb again. Dave glimpsed the fast-flowing river, racing white over glistening boulders.

Ahead of them, to the left, there were swaths cut through the woods that must have been downhill runs for skiing.

On the first of the sharp bends, the pavement was split by quakes and ice into a jagged crevasse, two feet wide and nearly as deep. Lee had no chance.

The front wheels of the Trackbreaker hit the hole with a sickening jolt, and they heard the double thump of the tires blowing.

As they rolled to a grinding halt, Dave sighed. "Time to walk," he said quietly.

4

"I'm real sorry, Dad."

Dave shook his head. "You apologize one more time about it, Lee, and I swear I'll kick your butt clear into the river!"

"But I should've seen—"

"No! There wasn't any way you could possibly have guessed that bastard crevasse was waiting for us around a blind curve."

Zera gazed back up at the road as it snaked high above them. "Would have been better if the tires had gone when we were at the top."

"Sure." Lee grinned. "I'll try harder next time."

Dave looked at the front of the Trackbreaker. He kicked disconsolately at the broken wheels, amazed the axle hadn't also gone. The damage was the kind that Robby's Auto Shop in Cody Heights would have fixed for him in an hour or so.

"Best start some unloading," he said in a resigned voice.

"What do we take?" Zera asked as she reached down to pat Melmoth on the head. The pit bull seemed to realize that some disaster had struck, and was wandering around, keeping close to one of them at all times.

"What we need and what we can carry—if they come to be the same."

"Least we cut down when we dumped the trailer back at Granny's place."

"Now we have to cut down a lot more. The same as survival backpacking."

"Sleeping bags and rucksacks," said Zera. "How 'bout food?"

Dave rubbed absently at the stubble along the line of his jawbone. "Not too much. We're going to go back to hunting again."

Lee smiled, then did a credible imitation of his father. "We've done it before and we'll do it again."

Dave patted him on the arm. "Sure. Let's get to it."

They busied themselves by sifting through the vehicle's contents. One of the biggest problems was trying to decide just what to take in the weaponry line. Guns weighed heavy, and so did ammo.

"Can't realistically hope to catch up with Sheever unless we travel fast and light," Dave mused.

"But we can't hope to beat the shit out of his gang unless we have the firepower."

Dave looked at Zera. "True. So, like everything else in this fucked-up world, we'll have to find the right compromise to keep us alive."

In the end, they didn't leave much behind.

Dave hung on to his Linebaugh .475, which was built onto a Ruger Bisley Blackhawk frame. Zera kept the nickel-plated .32 Ruger that had once belonged to Janine Rand. And Lee had the 9 mm SIG-Sauer 232 pistol. All of them carried on the hip.

Dave decided they should drop off one of the shotguns, another one, a rifle. Despite Lee's protests, the Onyx was broken over a large boulder and left in fragments.

"It was a birthday present, Dad."

"You were also given that antique Ninja Turtle toy by Aunt Rose. You can't carry the past with you, son. I'm sorry."

That left Dave to heft the Browning 12-gauge, while Zera insisted on taking over the Skorpion Mk 3 machine pistol.

It was difficult to decide between the Heckler & Koch G12 caseless and the Sauer 120 Lux rifle. The availability of ammunition finally made Dave grudgingly pick the .458 eight-round rifle with the Leupold optical sight.

Zera shot Dave a questioning look. "What about the longbows? They're not too heavy."

"Yeah. Guess we could probably carry them strapped over the shoulders."

"One should be enough," Lee said. "Say, a dozen arrows. Can't honestly see how we'd need any more."

"True. All right. And we've got our knives?"

Lee showed his Mamba Blackjack. "And I've also got the short-handled ax."

"Zera?"

"Got this." She held up a thin-bladed flensing knife with a taped hilt.

"Fine. I've got the machete and the 10-inch Trailmaster knife. That's it."

"What about my Smith & Wesson 12-gauge?" said the young woman.

Dave sighed. "Damned if I hadn't forgotten that. Bit heavy for you, along with the other firepower. Best we ditch it."

"I'd rather keep it."

The man suddenly realized they were heading for a showdown. Zera was challenging his authority as leader of the group.

"No. We've got enough to take on Sheever. With the size of the party he's leading, we'd never hope to win a straightforward firefight anyway."

Her blue eyes open wide, Zera faced him, cradling the scattergun in her arms. Dave noticed with a frisson of fear that her index finger was on the trigger. Lee took a half step forward, then froze.

"What if I say I'm keeping it, Dave? What happens then?"

"Then you keep it."

She nodded, half-smiling. "Thought you might see it my way."

"Yeah," he went on. "You keep the gun and you go your own way."

"Dad!" Lee gasped.

"That's how it is. I'll listen to both your views on any subject you like. When it comes to the rock wall, then my word holds."

"I see."

Dave held her with his eyes, solemn and calm. "So, you dump the shotgun and come with us, Zera? Or you walk away."

"Bastard," she said quietly. "I'd taken a liking to it."

She swung the weapon against a large boulder at the side of the highway, breaking off the folding stock. Then she kicked the remnants over the edge, into the river.

"We got to sort out what food we take and all the rest of the stuff," said Dave. "Let's get moving as

fast as we can. Now we've closed the gap this much
I don't want to let them slip far ahead of us again.''

They were almost ready to go, and stood looking at the Trackbreaker. It was a temptation to
torch the four-by and give it the blazing send-off
that it deserved. But if they could see the smoke
from what was probably Sheever's fire, then he
would easily see the towering pillar of darkness that
would burst from the Trackbreaker.

The vehicle was now unusable. But if anyone
came along who had the technical skill to repair it
and get it back on the road . . .

"Then, good luck to them," said Dave.

AFTER THE SOFT DAYS of riding on four wheels,
they found it hard work to walk on under the heavy
packs.

By the time they'd struggled to the crest of the
road, the sunlight had vanished, and threatening
purple clouds were raging in from the north. The
temperature had fallen by at least fifteen degrees,
and the first flakes of snow started whirling about
them.

Dave felt as though a tight band of steel was
shrinking around his chest, making it difficult to
breathe. Twice he had to stop, going down onto his
knees on a sharp bend, fighting for control. Tiny
black specks flickered in front of his eyes, and the

dancing whorls of snow made him feel as though he were on a merry-go-round.

"Shit! I'm so out of condition. Have to take five when we get to the top."

Lee grinned. "Sure you don't want me and Zera to carry on without you? We could always try and send a stretcher back for you."

Dave threw his son the finger. "I'll get there. Might have to load my pack onto Melmoth . . . but I'll get there."

Zera strode out with little apparent effort, her long legs taking her up the rutted, broken highway. As they walked, there was ample evidence they were closer to the group of horsemen than they'd ever been before. The track was dotted with horse droppings.

Dave stirred one pile with the toe of his Danner boot, peering at it. "Only a few hours old," he said.

"You're an expert on horseshit now," said Zera, smiling at him.

"Couple of years ago and I didn't know diddly about horseshit. And baby, look at me now."

There was still more proof of how close they were to the Sheever gang when they reached the site of the camp fire. It was in a clearing, overlooking the river valley far below. Dave shrugged off his pack, glad of the chance to take a break. He knelt to feel the ashes, and pulled his hand back quickly. "Still real hot," he said.

Scattered around the place were the ragged remains of a deer's carcass. Gnawed bones were silent evidence of serious hunger in Sheever's group. It had already occurred to Dave that traveling through the ravaged land with so many people and animals would raise major problems of logistics in food and drink.

The same thing had preoccupied Lee. "They must be spending a whole lot of time hunting," he said. "Have to send some of them on ahead to try and get game. Looks like they don't have too much."

The pit bull had found enough to satisfy himself, grinding at shreds of meat attached to a pair of the deer's ribs.

"How far behind them do you think we are?" asked Zera, squatting on her heels. Dave felt vaguely irritated that she didn't even feel the need to slip her pack off.

"This must be their night fire. It's early afternoon now. Can't be more than six hours from them. Trouble is... they'll be able to move a lot faster than we can on foot. I can't go on much farther today. Means they're slipping away."

"How far to that canyon place where they're going to hole up?"

Dave looked at his son. "You've got the map. Or have I got it?"

He had it himself, tucked into one of the zipped pockets at the front of his pack. The wind was rising, and it proved difficult to read, the edges fluttering. "We're about here," Dave said, pointing with a gloved finger. "That's the bend where the tires went. The river. Wait a minute. Something... Looks like the river used to flow at a different angle, coming in from over that far side. There must have been a big land shift here."

"Where's this canyon place?" asked Zera, hunching her shoulders against the snow, which had at last begun to fall from the dull, leaden sky with a real purpose.

Dave jabbed at the map. "Ski resort there, and it's beyond it. But this map could prove to be way out."

Lee was rubbing his hands together against the chill. "Anything between us and them? Some sort of shelter or something?"

"Nothing. Wait... no, I'm wrong. Little settlement over the far side of this ridge. About ten miles away. Called—" he brought the map closer to his face "—my sight's not what it was. Yeah, here it is.

Called Altmann. Then it's another forty miles to Castle Ridge. That must be the box canyon, just beyond it, up that stream."

"What's that?"

"What?"

Lee pointed at a crosshatched line that ran down the far side of the mountain from them. "There's a lot of them."

"Ski lifts," said Dave, after some hesitation and peering at the key.

"Shame they aren't working. Be nice to get up and down that easy." Zera smiled. "Used to ski some at college."

"I did some on a high school trip. Dad used to be good, didn't you?"

"I got by."

Lee slapped his father on the shoulder, rocking him on his heels. "Double-modest! You made the Olympic team, didn't you? On the downhill?"

Dave straightened. "Nearly. Kind of reserve." He folded the map and replaced it safely in his pack, then hefted the weight on his shoulders again with a groan. "Come on, folks. Time to move on."

Within the hour the snow had reached blizzard proportions and visibility was down to less than fifty feet. They could still make out the trail between the trees, and Dave's compass told them they were moving in the right direction. But darkness would soon be stalking them, and Dave Rand knew one thing for sure.

If they didn't find shelter quickly, the next dawn could see them dead.

5

The night came out of the mountains and swooped down on them, folding them into the black wings of its cape.

Darkness caught them still struggling along the ridge above the Sheever campsite. The terrain showed evidence of one of the eruptions that had sent great bursts of molten rock for more than one hundred miles across the northern states, turning rivers to steam and stripping trees to charred stumps a few inches high.

The trail was already vanishing under the layer of fresh snow. Dave had kept moving, head down, checking every few paces that the others were with him. From everything he remembered from his survival training, he knew they were already into high risk. Hypothermia was waiting, grinning wolfishly, ready for them to become tired. Waiting for them to decide it really wouldn't do any harm to lie down and take a small rest.

Lee was carrying the tent, and his father waited for him to catch up, then shouted at the top of his voice to be heard above the wail of the wind. "Have to rest up!"

"Tent'll never hold out there."

Zera appeared from what was fast becoming a lethal whiteout. Her face was crusted with snow and beads of glistening ice hung from her eyes, nose and lips. "Hard going," she said, panting.

Dave closed his eyes for a moment, trying to concentrate. The gale numbed the senses and the mind, making it immensely difficult to fight toward the right decision.

"Got to stop. Find shelter."

"Where?"

"Map showed ski lifts. Can't be far."

Zera tugged at his arm. "Why can't we put up the tent?"

"Wind's too strong. Nothing to hold it down. If it blew away, we'd be stone dead."

"So we go on . . . until . . ."

Dave punched her on the arm, hard enough to rock her on her feet. "We go on until we find some place safe to hole up until the storm's done. That all right with you, Zera?"

"Bastard," she said, with no real anger. She plodded on, trying to fit her feet into the tracks he was leaving. At a nod from his father, Lee Rand started trudging along, bringing up the rear.

The ground was sloping down, but visibility had dropped to zero. Dave fumbled along, hands out in front of him. Lee hung on to his belt, and Zera hung on to Lee's belt.

Melmoth was surprisingly unfazed by the desperate weather. He would scamper along in front of them, plowing through the belly-deep drifts, vanish for several minutes, then reappear, his coat matted with snow. But suddenly Dave was aware that the pit bull had been gone for longer than usual on his forays. Now, in the blindingly white darkness, time was also vanishing.

Wearily, Dave was starting to think it might be all right if they just stopped for a few minutes. "Catch our breath," he said, licking ice from the corners of his mouth.

Then Melmoth bounded from the swirling snow, darting around his feet, barking excitedly. The pit bull ran ahead again and disappeared once more, his yapping drowned in the muffling wind.

Lee pulled hard on his father's belt, halting him. "Melmoth's found something, Dad," he yelled, bringing his mouth close to Dave's ear. "Stick with him."

There wasn't much else to do.

They were vaguely aware that they'd moved out of the area of bleak desolation and were now once more among trees. Clumps of piñon pines lined the trail, giving shelter from both snow and wind.

To the left Dave glimpsed the stark outline of a rusting pylon, with a length of cable snaking elegantly from its top into the snow beneath. And a little farther on, beyond a second pylon, he saw the squat shape of a small building.

With the hope of shelter and rest so close, exhaustion clawed at his legs, turning every step into an exercise in pain. The snow pattered into his face, making him blink. Lee's hand at his belt seemed to drag him down.

The door was closed, and Dave fumbled for what seemed a freezing eternity to open it. When the catch wouldn't respond to his thick gloves, he pounded at it in anger and despair. Zera pushed past him, her fingers bare, and easily turned the handle, heaving the door open. She helped Dave in, Lee at her heels, Melmoth darting in between them.

"Close it," she said, panting, allowing Dave to drop to his knees in the center of the room.

The silence immediately swam about them, muting their world after the storm's passion.

Lee wriggled out of his pack quickly and immediately went to his father to squat at his side. "You all right, Dad?"

"Oh, Jesus! I feel sick as a dog. Sorry, Melmoth. Don't know what...like the past few days all caught up with... with me at once. I'll be okay.... Help me off with my pack, will you?"

It was dark in the hut, but Zera found a switch and threw it. Like most mountain survival shelters, this one had its own battery-storage system. A pale, forty-watt bulb came on, pushing the storm even farther away.

The hut contained a table, two chairs and six bunks, ranged around the walls in pairs. On one wall was a fireplace and chimney. A cooking stove sat in a corner, connected by a hose to a portable gas cylinder. Two shelves held a number of boxes and packets that immediately took Lee's interest. In a jiffy he was happily rummaging through the supplies.

"Soup and vegetables and some stews. Puddings. Tea. Sugar and freeze-dried milk. This is heaven!"

"Get a fire going, Lee. Need to have the place warmed up some. There's kindling and wood by the hearth."

Over the mantel they saw a large printed notice, faded and dog-eared, and draped with a complex spiderweb.

This is an emergency relief shelter, to be used only by those in serious need. It is checked every four days by rangers, and anyone contravening the above will be liable to prosecution under state and federal legislation. Theft from this or any shelter is punishable by fines and, in some cases, imprisonment.

Supplies are replenished every four days. If you use wood, please replace it before you leave, if possible. There are flares on the shelf above the stove. Use gas sparingly. Contributions toward the upkeep of this shelter may be made by mail to...

Someone had torn that corner off the notice, but the travelers now had warm thoughts for the rangers. It was clear they had just had a close call with white, silent death.

"IF WE WEREN'T in such a hurry, we'd hole up here for a couple of days," said Dave. "Recharge our own batteries."

A fire blazed in the hearth, sending sparks fountaining up the chimney. Melmoth, half-asleep, lay stretched contentedly in front of it. The table held the remains of their meal: beef stew, vegetables cooked in mushroom soup, a kind of custard with bits of fruit chopped into it, with mugs of sweet milky coffee to follow.

Dave relaxed in one of the top bunks, under a couple of blankets, feeling warm and comfortable for the first time in months. From outside, barely audible above the crackling of the pine logs, came the sound of the raging storm.

Lee sat at the table, his head in his hands, gradually falling asleep. His eyes would blink shut, and his head would nod, then he'd jerk awake again. He'd stripped down to a thermal vest and jeans, stretching his bare feet toward the fire, but far enough away to remove the risk of chilblains.

Zera rested on a lower bunk, hugging the cooling remnants of her third mug of coffee. She wore a T-shirt untucked from her jeans. Like Lee she was barefoot.

Dave thought how attractive she looked and felt the familiar stirring as he glanced across the room at her. He wondered if she might come to him again in the night. The feeling of embarrassment because of the presence of his son was gone. Also, he'd come to realize, Lee slept the deep sleep of the young.

Still, it was something else that had changed in Dave—to make love to a young woman in the same room as Lee!

He deliberately shifted his mind and remarked, "Least those bastards'll have trouble moving through weather like this. Horses'll get spooked."

"So we could maybe rest a day or so?" asked Lee, stretching and yawning hugely.

"Yeah, we could. But we won't."

THE STORM DIDN'T EASE for nearly seventy-two hours. A couple of times it seemed to be quieting, and Lee and Dave went out for a few minutes to try to gather some wind-broken branches for the fire. But it always gathered strength again and snarled around the cabin, rattling the shutters over the small, deep-set windows.

The food supplies that had seemed more than ample were shrinking fast. Melmoth was clearly unhappy, pacing around in the cramped room, whining by the door. But when he was let out he walked only a few steps into the snow, did what he had to and came scurrying back to dry himself by the fire.

On the fourth day dawn broke dry and clear. Soon a bright sun was shining in a sky of unsullied blue, and the snow lay like a blanket of forgiveness over the bruised earth.

Zera was first up. She opened the door of the hut and whooped with delight. "Like a Christmas card!

Come on, you lazy bastards! Let's get up and going."

The snow was piled all around, against the wooden walls of the shelter. Even among the trees there were drifts, and snow lay like foam along the stark branches. The temperature was still below freezing, but the near-hurricane wind had been tempered to a pleasant light breeze. Without the wind, walking would be almost enjoyable.

As soon as he saw the beautiful morning, Dave was out of his bunk, wincing slightly as he found himself still stuck to part of the gray blanket. As he hastily dressed, he was also very aware of the scent of Zera clinging to his body.

"How far do you reckon we are behind them, Dad?" asked Lee. "A half day or so?"

"Probably about that. But from this moment on, they can go faster than us. Through this snow, it'll be slow walking."

"Isn't that small town somewhere around here?"

Dave nodded at Zera's question. "Altmann? Yeah. Should be only a few miles from here."

He walked outside, taking deep breaths, relishing the freshness after three days stuck in the close confines of the hut. Dave glanced behind him at the shelter, only too aware that they would certainly have died without it.

"What the...?" he said to himself, as he noticed another building, set behind the cabin. Smaller and lower without any windows. He called to the others. "Hey, look!"

"What?"

"Round here. Some kind of store. It's got a real big padlock and steel bar. Haven't been touched."

Lee and Zera joined him, Melmoth wading determinedly behind them.

Dave rattled the lock. "We're lucky Sheever stuck to the main highway and missed this place."

"How do we get in?"

"Give me the ax."

Dave hefted the ax, turning it so that the back of the blade would hit the edge of the padlock. He struck a single, sharp blow. The ringing of metal on metal was followed by a loud click as the lock sprang open.

"Nice one," said Zera, clapping her hands admiringly. "Sure you majored in double-entry bookkeeping and not single-entry housebreaking?"

The bar swung out of the way, and Dave tugged at the door handle. The hinges needed oil, and they gave a hideous screech, like that of a tormented bird. Melmoth barked at the sudden noise.

"Quiet, boy, quiet. There's no light inside. Pull the door all the way open."

Three immaculate snowmobiles were lined up, their Plexiglas shields showing through a layer of dust. Lee whooped in delight, and Dave, too, couldn't conceal his pleasure at their find.

Unfortunately, there was no gas in the tanks and no containers of gas to be seen. But leaning against the walls were dozens of pairs of skis and a couple of small towing sleds.

"Could've been better," said Zera.

Dave was busily trying on skis. "And it could have been a lot worse."

6

Altmann, Montana, Snowmobile Capital of the United States, Population 4576. Elevation 4223 Feet above Sea Level. Watch your speed and drive friendly.

In the white space at the bottom of the sign, partly worn away but still legible, was spray-painted: Exercise Your Right to Vote. Elect Tanner for '49.

It was not far from evening when Dave, Lee and Zera reached the first abandoned buildings on the outskirts of the little town. Beyond the large sign they had just read, and between two speed-limit signs they saw a rectangular board with "Altmann, Montana, Twin Town with Nashville, Tennessee" in large, Gothic-style, gold lettering. Someone had taken a dislike to the sign and hit it with a burst of automatic fire, and the cluster of bullets all within the space of a man's hand had eliminated part of the word *Twin*.

Dave looked at the damage, noting the fresh white edges to the splintered holes. "Been done within the past day or so," he remarked.

"Sheever?" asked Lee, resting on his ski poles.

"Has to be."

Melmoth was sitting in regal splendor on the back of the sled hauled by Dave. He stared around him with a grand disdain. Early in the afternoon they'd first seen signs that they were again on the trail of the mounted gang, and the pit bull had then shown some interest. Now, however, he was looking bored.

"We going to go straight in?" asked Lee.

"No. Sheever and his men might still be there. He doesn't know us...doesn't know we're after him. But the girls might see us and give everything away."

Zera sniffed, wiping her nose on her sleeve. "That mean you'd like me to go in first?"

"Yes, it's the only way that makes sense. Lee and I'll wait here for you. Best take your skis in with you. Tell them you're with a biggish party, and you are trekking westward. That way they shouldn't take a chance on hassling you."

"Should she take the guns with her, Dad?"

"Yeah, or maybe just take in the .32 Ruger. Keep it in your belt."

"Sure. How long are you going to give me, before you come in like the Marines to rescue me?"

Dave checked his watch. "It'll be dark in less than an hour."

"And getting seriously cold," Lee put in. "Maybe we ought to try and find some place to hole up for the night. Then Zera could go in at first light."

Dave considered his son's suggestion and saw it made a lot of sense. To have the young woman wandering around in pitch-black night wasn't the greatest idea. "Right," he said. "Let's move in slow and careful and find somewhere to sleep."

MANY OF THE outlying buildings in Altmann had been broken into and their contents taken. But the shells of the houses still remained, with only doors or windows damaged. There was no sign of the wanton destruction and arson that they'd seen in other settlements.

Dave picked a single-story house with a high-pitched roof, standing alone up a side road. It overlooked the town but was secluded behind a wall of mature trees and shrubs. The back door had been kicked in and everything inside reduced to a tumbled mess of furniture and a few clothes. It didn't take them long to hang drapes over the windows that faced Altmann and then start a roaring fire in the grate.

Lee went out to answer a call of nature and came back to report both light and noise coming from the buildings below them.

"Shouting and singing," he said. "And I could smell food cooking. Why can't we go on down there now? See what's happening?"

"No. In the morning," replied Dave. "We start taking chances, and we'll end up taking one too many. In the morning will be good enough."

ZERA CAME QUIETLY to Dave in the night, wriggling warm and sinuous into the sleeping bag. Her fingers roused him and guided him into her waiting body. Dave kept his eyes squeezed shut, closing out his son, who was sleeping only a few feet away from them, his face ruddy in the glow of the dying fire.

As he thrust his way toward a climax, Dave suddenly caught an errant memory of his dead wife, Janine, sitting by the fire in their old home, reading a novel. Her eyes lifting to his, and a half smile touching her lips.

For a moment he hesitated, feeling himself begin to shrink. Zera responded to the pause, holding him tighter, the tip of her tongue touching his ear. She whispered, "Want to stop a bit?"

"No. No."

He recovered, grinding down into the girl's compliant body, aware of her breathing faster, her thighs squeezing him, the muscles of her body drawing him into her warm depths.

"Oh, yes, Dave, yes." The words were so soft they barely reached him.

Afterward, Zera returned to her own sleeping bag, leaving Dave alone.

Very alone.

DAWN BROUGHT SNOW.

Thick driving flakes swept in from the mountains to the west, blanketing the trails and piling up at the front of the house. Visibility was less than ten yards. Melmoth had to be pushed out the door to go and do his business, and he came quickly back, whining and snarling.

Zera wrapped herself up and buckled on her skis. She gave Dave a quick kiss on the cheek, her lips cold against his skin. "Be back soon," she said.

"Snow'll cover your tracks double-fast," said Lee. "But you better be careful coming back here. Don't want a bunch of town crazies on your heels."

"Sure," she said, looked at Dave for a second, then she was gone, soundless in the blizzard, vanishing before she reached the first of the looming trees.

Dave closed the front door against the driving snow. There was nothing left to do but wait.

Around nine Melmoth started to growl. He ran to the side of the house, where a broken pool table stood on three crooked legs. Lee snatched up the Skorpion, cocking it as he moved through the shadowy hall. Dave, Linebaugh in his fist, followed right behind.

"Quiet!" whispered the boy, kneeling by the window. He patted the pit bull on the back. Cautiously he raised his head and peered outside.

Dave was flattened against the wall of the main entrance hall. "See anything?"

"No. Just a mess of snow."

"Something spooked Melmoth."

"There's...it's a dog. A scrawny mongrel, its ribs sticking out."

"Just one dog?"

"Yeah. Should I shoot it?"

"No. No reason."

"It's going."

"Good. Sure there's nobody with it?"

Lee turned back from the smeared glass. "Nothing. Look, Melmoth's quieted. Hey, Dad?"

"What?"

"Can I light the fire?"

"No. If the snow clears suddenly, they'd be able to see smoke from town."

"I'm cold, Dad."

"Try some exercises, son. Best I can suggest. If we're still here after dark, we'll break up some more of the furniture and have a fire."

Lee left the room, walking slowly along the hall into the living room. The dog followed him, his claws clicking on the smooth wooden tiles.

Dave watched them and shook his head in the icy cavern. His son was growing fast. He was taller and stronger than he'd been when the asteroid hit. Now he was built like a man, inches over six feet and broadening at the shoulder. But his face had aged most. The eyes weren't those of a boy of sixteen. They were deep-set and cold, often seeming to be looking far beyond the present into some grim unknowable future.

THE SNOW STOPPED falling a little after noon. The low cloud cover eased away on the back of a freshening wind, revealing shreds of blue sky. The new snow lay pure and even, unmarked by any tracks. Dave wondered whether he should go after Zera. If Sheever and his gang of psychopaths were still in Altmann, then her life might be at risk.

"No choice," he said.

"How do you mean, Dad?" asked Lee, coming in from the front porch.

"Didn't even know I'd spoken out loud. Sure sign I'm turning into a geriatric total."

"Can I go look for Zera?"

"No." Dave pointed outside. "Light's good, and against this blanket of white, anyone moving'd stand out like..."

"Dog shit on a wedding cake," suggested Lee with a broad grin.

"Something like that."

It was less than a half hour later when at last Zera reappeared.

Her anorak was torn, and she'd clearly been crying. Before they got to her, she came to a neat halt, stooping to unbuckle the skis. She saw the question in Dave's face and called out the answer.

"Yeah, they were here. Left a day ago. And the girls were with them."

Dave Rand slowly unclenched his fingers, looking incuriously at the marks his nails had left in his palms.

"A day ago," he said.

7

"Give anything for a real keying great vodka," Zera said with a little tremor in her voice.

She tried for a smile and fell a country mile short. Her lip began to tremble, and fresh tears started to trickle over her cheeks. As she pulled off the hood of the anorak, Dave and Lee saw a bruise under her left eye and a thread of dried blood running from the corner of her mouth.

"Sheever?" asked Dave quietly.

She took several slow, shuddering breaths, managing to regain control. "Like I said, he went off with most of his men and took your daughters with him."

"So what fucker did this to you?"

"I said most of his men. Not all. There's a couple of real nice mothers still in town."

"Did they...?" Dave found that he somehow couldn't complete the question.

Zera touched the swelling around her eye. Shook her head and gave him a brief cold smile. "Fuck me? No. They were both too fucking drunk to fuck anyone. They just roughed me up some. Didn't like my haircut. Didn't like the way I looked at them. It was the old whore that got the fuckers off me."

"Whore? What do you mean?"

"I mean whore, Dave, as in prostitute. Someone who peddles herself for money. Or, in the case of the Altmann brothel, for anything that'll pass for trade. Food and liquor score high."

"I don't get it," he said.

Zera told Lee and Dave a little more about the setup in town while resting to recover from her ordeal.

What was left of Altmann after the Big Hit seemed to be little more than a thriving brothel called the Black Hole, in what had once been a run-down hotel on the town's main street. It was operated by a middle-aged woman whose name, Zera thought, was Nancy.

"All very neat and tidy," she said. "Bar along one wall and a sort of waiting-room place with big chairs and a couple of maroon sofas. It was odd...it looked just like a brothel in some old vid."

"And the girls go for trade?" asked Lee.

"Yeah. I saw one guy come in with a string of fish in a basket. Won himself twenty minutes with one of the women. Nancy seemed to set a tariff off the top of her head."

Dave got up and walked to stare out the window at the bright, sunny afternoon. "And Sheever and my girls?"

Zera stood up and joined him. "Nobody followed me, if that's what you're worrying about. Both the thugs were too drunk to walk straight, never mind come skiing up a mountain."

"The girls?" he prompted.

"Yeah. Nancy told me they seemed to be well. Sort of thin, she said they were."

"How did you get the beating," asked Lee, who was sitting at a small table and field-stripping his SIG-Sauer .232 pistol.

"When I got into town—mostly closed up and deserted—I saw the Black Hole and went in. It was quiet, with only three girls, Nancy and these two men, both in camouflage gear, dripping guns and knives. Nancy came straight over and tried to warn me off. I had time to ask her real quietly about Sheever, and she began to tell me. Then Ugly One and Ugly Two saw me and started in. They got rough but Nancy helped me away without any real harm. I was worried most they'd find the Ruger. I thought about taking them out with it. I could've done it, Dave."

Her voice trembled again, and he put an arm across her shoulders. "Sure. But I'm glad you didn't. I might want a word with them."

"What guns'll we take, Dad?"

Dave pointed at Lee's 9 mm handgun. "That. And I'll take the Linebaugh."

"I'll bring the Ruger," Zera volunteered.

"You stay here. Keep an eye on Melmoth for us."

"I'm coming."

"Best you stay," he insisted, but saw by the stubborn look in her eyes that this time she wouldn't take no for an answer.

They chose to walk, rather than burden themselves with unwieldy skis. The snow was smooth, no more than seven or eight inches deep. Apart from the menacing drifts piled to a height of several feet along the highway and on the windward flanks of the buildings of Altmann, the weather was no threat.

Melmoth kept close by them. The snow was deep enough to make walking uncomfortable for him. He whined miserably as he plowed through a deeper patch, making Lee laugh at him.

"Cold enough to freeze the balls off a brass pit bull," he sniggered.

The dog turned on the boy and snarled at him, baring his teeth.

"Jesus, Melmoth! It was only a joke."

They soon reached the main street. It approached the town through a sharp left turn, then straightened past a row of abandoned stores. Dave held them back at the turn, looking round the corner, and immediately seeing the Black Hole. As Zera had said, it had obviously once been a hotel, and still had a seedy portico over the main entrance.

"Okay, if we go in there together, it'll look suss. Since it's a brothel, it'll look reasonable if I go in first."

"What are you going to offer for trade? They don't take old dollars."

Dave wiped sweat from his forehead. It was one of the warmest days he could remember for months. The sun was throwing sharp-edged shadows across the untouched shroud of whiteness.

"Melmoth," he said.

"Oh, Dad!" exclaimed Lee. "You can't trade him in for... for a woman!"

"Lee, I'm not really going to trade him. I sometimes think you left the better part of your brains back in Cody Heights. It's just for cover, so I can get in and see these guys."

"Then what?" Zera demanded.

Dave had been asking himself that same question all the way down from the house where they spent the night. And he hadn't really come up with a good answer.

"Talk to 'em, I guess. Ask them a couple of questions. That's all."

"What about us?" Lee asked.

"Wait here. They've already seen Zera, and they might start shooting if they see us all coming in. Wait here and cover me. Any firing, come running and make sure you got your guns ready."

"Careful, Dad," muttered the boy, kneeling to pat Melmoth.

"Yeah. Los Bros Ugly aren't very nice, Dave. Get your retaliation in first."

DAVE RAND HADN'T SEEN so many people in one place since before Adastreia terminated civilization.

The air smelled stale and heavy from drinking, and there was a blue-gray haze of smoke. His nose also detected the herbal scent of dope. The lobby was just the way Zera had described it. A long mahogany bar, metal-topped, with a patterned mirror running the full length. Behind it was an array of dusty bottles, most of them nearly empty.

About a dozen men sat at small tables, smoking and drinking, a few of them playing a quiet but intense game of cards. They all wore the same kind of clothes, a mix of patched furs and hiking gear. Dave immediately spotted four rifles and a brace of scatterguns. But there was no sign of the two men in camouflage tops and pants.

Heads turned as he pushed through the doors into the fug of sweat and smoke. Dave stood still, aware that it was best not to draw any special attention to himself. The big Linebaugh was tucked into the top of his pants, under his anorak.

He saw the room beyond the bar, and the three women there, sitting talking under the flickering light of what had once been a wonderful crystal chandelier. But it was missing fully half of the glittering drops. The scene was so much like one in an old vid that it took several seconds before Dave realized the place was actually using electricity. In the background, he caught the faint hum of a gas generator.

"Looking for ladies, Mister?"

The men's heads had turned away, the card game had been resumed, as everyone lost interest in the stranger. Everyone except the woman who stood at Dave's side, a thin black cigar in one hand and an ivory-topped cane in the other. She looked about fifty, with iron-gray hair pinned back in a roll. Her ankle-length dress was dark green satin, tight at the waist. Her eyes were a watery blue, and she was squinting a little.

"Who are you?" asked Dave.

"Name's Nancy. The Black Hole's my place. I'll ask you again, have you come for my girls?"

"I'd like a word first."

"Talk's free here, Mister. A piece of action comes rather more costly."

Mclmoth was on a leash, and he pushed forward, sniffing at the madam's ankles. She looked down at him and smiled. "That bastard bites me, and he's tomorrow's chili."

A voice spoke up from behind David Rand. "Dog like that bites you, and it could be you in the stew, Nancy."

The newcomer was a short black man, dressed in what had once been a smart business suit, which looked incongruous above a pair of stout walking boots. He wore rimless glasses, with one of the lenses starred across its center.

"You just keep your fucking nose out of my business, Doc."

He grinned at her, making a mocking half bow to Dave Rand. "See how even the mightiest are fallen, Mr. . . . ?"

"Henderson, Peter Henderson. I'm from San Francisco, originally."

"Dr. Edwin Kael," the black man volunteered. "Once the jewel in the medical crown of the Rose McLaren Hospital in Seattle. Now a pox doctor to this crone and her trio of scabby whores."

Melmoth continued to sniff at the woman's ankles. She looked down at him again and said, "I'd like you to take that animal out of the Black Hole, Mr. Henderson, before he scares the shit out of me and my customers. Speaking of which, are you a customer?"

Dave looked away. "Well . . ."

"No reason for embarrassment here," Edwin Kael said with a short laugh.

"I hear you don't take money," said Dave.

"Guns. Food. Drink. Liquor's specially good. Bring me in a couple of fifths of decent whiskey, and you can have all three girls take you around the world and back again."

"I was sort of hoping to trade in the dog here for a spin."

Nancy laughed, hands on hips, showing a set of perfect teeth. The others in the place looked up toward her, then went back to their own business. Dave glanced in the direction of the staircase, thinking he'd spotted movement, but nothing was stirring in the shadows now.

"Well, you got bigger balls than this pit bull of yours. Thanks, but no thanks. Will I take him? The hell, I will."

Suddenly Dave decided he'd had enough of game playing.

"Nancy," he said, keeping his voice quiet.

"What is it, Mister?"

The doctor looked at him, then nodded to himself and slowly headed for the bar.

"My name's Rand. Dave Rand."

"So? You still don't get laid here unless you got a way of paying for it."

"Suppose you had a couple of guests you wanted moving on?"

She looked at him sharply, half turned toward the stairs, then checked herself. "Ah," she said, "that young woman who came in earlier. Some relation?"

"No. But you're on the right road. Two girls who were held prisoner by the big blond man."

"Sheever."

"You know the girls I—"

"Your daughters." There was no question in the voice.

"It's a long story, Nancy, but I'm after them. I hear two of his men are here. Up the stairs. I need to talk to these guys."

"Mister . . . I don't hear you and I don't see you. Fact is, I've never seen you and maybe I never will. You understand me? I tell you this. That yellow-haired giant is the most swift and evil bastard I have ever seen in my life. And I've seen some honey peaches. The guys are in room 6. End of the corridor. Both got some serious guns with them."

"Drunk?"

She considered the question. "Some."

"Why are they staying here?"

Nancy shook her head. "Who knows? Maybe some sort of a falling-out with Sheever. Lot of them are army, you know. They'd had enough of horse riding. I think they figured on catching up later."

"Know where?"

"No. Do you?"

"Box canyon beyond Castle Ridge. I need to know more."

"Go ask. But remember what I said. If they send you off on the last train west, I've never seen you before."

"All right if I leave the dog down here? I'll tie him to the table."

Nancy nodded her reluctant agreement and turned away in a flounce of satin.

As Dave started up the creaking staircase, the doctor turned from the bar and raised a shot glass to him.

8

The Black Hole was appropriately named.

Despite months of living virtually without a bath or a good wash, Dave Rand found his nostrils wrinkling at the stink that hovered in the corridor at the top of the stairs. It was mainly the stink of unwashed bodies, with the odors of every other possible human activity mixing in the brew. There was also the greasy smell of fried food, rancid and sickening.

Dave drew the Linebaugh from his belt, cocking it ready. Room 2 faced him and room 3 was next along to the left. He turned right, stepping lightly on what remained of a torn and faded runner. The passage was gloomy with only a single window at its farther end admitting a watery light.

Room 5 lacked a door. He glanced in at it as he walked by, saw a broken bed and a pile of clothes, then realized the clothes covered a limp human form. From ahead he could catch the faint sound of voices. Behind him the building was silent as a tomb.

He paused for a moment, gathering himself. Unbidden, a memory surfaced of his old lecturer in Business Efficiency. Ed Sirak. He'd always said, "Have a plan. If you have a plan you'll win the day."

Dave realized that he didn't have any sort of plan. Kick open the door and then . . .

"Then?" he whispered.

A bellow of laughter from room 6 brought him sharply back to the present. He inched along, keeping near the right-hand wall. A framed print of a wrecked sailing ship hung crookedly there, and Dave resisted the temptation to straighten it.

Five more steps, then four.

The door ahead of him swung open, and a dark figure came stumbling out, head thrown back, roaring with laughter.

"So he slapped both handfuls up—"

As he began to turn, he suddenly noticed Dave standing there, holding the cannon of a revolver.

"You—" Dave began. But the man was quicker than he'd expected, spinning toward him rather than trying to dodge away, a slim-bladed knife appearing out of nowhere in his right hand.

There was the whisper of steel slicing through cloth and Dave felt a flash of fire along his left arm. He instinctively took a pace back, finger tight on the trigger of the Linebaugh, knowing that if he squeezed it he was likely to break his own wrist.

"Joe! Out here!" yelled the man, grinning wolfishly at Dave, revealing jagged stained teeth.

Again the knife darted toward Dave, and he took another step back along the corridor, feeling warm blood trickling down his arm and over the fingers of his left hand. The light was so poor that the man's camouflage jacket seemed to make his outline blurred. He was of average height with ragged hair over his shoulders.

"What the fuck's goin' on?" came a thin, reedy voice from inside the room.

Time seemed to expand, making everything happen very slowly. Dave heard bed springs creak as the second of Sheever's thugs swung his feet to the floor.

"No fucking balls, you dirty prick," said the knifeman, flicking the blade from hand to hand, feinting at Dave with it. "And that's how you'll finish . . . I'll hack 'em off you."

The dancing steel kept Dave going backward, level with the gaping doorway of room 5. A second man emerged from room 6, holding a machine pistol.

"Shit," said Dave. He leaped sideways into the wrecked bedroom, as though he were terrified. But the moment he was out of sight he dropped into a shooter's crouch, bracing his right wrist with his bloodied left hand.

He waited.

"What's he got?" came the high-pitched voice again. "Looked like the Lincoln Tunnel with a trigger on it."

"Big Magnum. But he hasn't used it. Means the skinny fucker won't."

The speaker immediately jumped into room 5's doorway, a thin, murderous smile pasted onto the unshaven face.

"Wrong," said Dave, following up immediately with the smooth action of the trigger, feeling the familiar, brutal kick that jarred clear to the shoulder.

In one of Dave's survivalist courses, the instructor, an ex-Marine, had taught combat shooting. Places to put a bullet to make sure your enemy was down and done for. Dave and the others, mainly white-collar professional men, had laughed in the bar afterward at the idea that any of them would ever actually need to see an enemy down and done.

"Middle chest," the instructor had said. "That way you got a margin of several inches all round your primary target that'll do serious damage. Miss a head shot by a few inches, and you're on your back looking up at the sky.''

"Middle chest," breathed Dave, as the man was hurled out of the doorway into the hall by the force of the massive .475, full metal jacket round.

The exit wound between the shoulders was the size of a dinner plate, spraying the wall of the corridor with blood and splintered bone. Before the dying man had slumped to the dusty floor, Dave powered after him into a diving roll on his left shoulder and up into a crouch.

Joe, holding an Uzi, was about ten feet away, silhouetted against the window. He was about five foot two, and wore only a torn denim shirt that barely covered his loins.

Aiming carefully, Dave pulled back on the trigger of the Linebaugh for the second time.

The handgun boomed, the sound echoing along the passage. The bullet passed clear through the little man's upper thigh, precisely where Dave had aimed, smashing the glass of the window.

Joe screamed, toppled sideways, but managed to hang on to the machine pistol, firing as he fell. Dave winced, closing his eyes in a reflex action as the hail of bullets raked the ceiling, bringing a blizzard of whirling plaster and lath splinters.

"Drop the gun, fuck head!" Dave shouted, ready to shoot again if he had to.

Immediately in front of him, the first of his victims was taking a noisy time in dying. A froth of blood was bubbling pinkly from the neat entrance hole just above his sternum. His legs were kicking a rattling tattoo on the linoleum, and his hands were clasped to his chest. His eyes were staring blindly into the empty room opposite him.

"Drop it!" Dave yelled, putting a third round a couple of inches above the head of the wounded Joe.

The Uzi clattered on the floor. Joe rolling to and fro, holding his shattered thigh, keeping up a ceaseless keening sound. Dave stood, slow and cautious, the hammer thumbed back. At his feet there was a sudden stillness as the first of Sheever's men entered the long night.

"Shut the fuck up," said Dave.

"You crippled me, you bitching bastard."

"Yeah."

"I'll never walk again."

"You'll never play the violin, either."

The man wriggled backward, so that he could lean against the wall, leaving a trail of blood. Dave was relieved to see that the main artery in the thigh hadn't been severed. He didn't want this one to die too fast.

"Why'd you come here and do this, Mister? What did we do to you?"

"Nothing."

"Then why?"

"Friend of mine from California, accountant like me, once deliberately slammed his dick shut in a filing cabinet. When he came out of hospital I asked him the same question. 'Why?' "

"Yeah?"

"He just said it seemed like a good idea at the time."

The man groaned in pain, face tight, not really listening to what Dave was saying. As he rolled, his shirt hiked up, revealing his shrunken genitals, splattered crimson.

"What's going on up there?"

"Don't worry, Nancy," called Dave.

"Anyone hurt?"

"One of your guests just checked out. The other one could be leaving soon."

"Need Doc Kael up there?"

"No," he said, then something occurred to him. "Hey, Nancy."

The madam answered, "What is it?"

"The young woman in here earlier—she and my son'll be arriving any minute now. They'll have heard the shooting."

"I'll take care of them, Mister. Sure you don't need anything?"

From the floor, the wounded man yelled along the corridor, "Get that nigger up here!"

A calm voice from the first floor answered him. "Nigger's busy drinking, Joe. Real sorry about that, brother."

Dave stood six feet away from Sheever's man, the Linebaugh steady on the man's naked belly.

"Just a few words," he said.

"Sheever'll hear about this, and he'll come back, and it'll be a fucking slow, hard passing, you back-shooting fucker!"

"Shouldn't worry you. You'll be dead and thrown out in the street long before then. But it's like you say, could be slow and hard."

"Fuck you!"

Dave didn't bother talking. He leveled the big handgun and put a bullet through the little man's left elbow, exploding the joint in a shambles of bone and muscle and tendons. The Linebaugh was so powerful that the single round almost severed the arm, leaving it dangling by frayed tendrils of flesh. Joe screamed and then passed out.

Dave sighed. While the man was unconscious, he took the time to carefully reload the Linebaugh, replacing the four discharged bullets, whose cases tinkled on the blood-slick floor.

"Dad!"

"Stay down there, Lee. I'm fine. Everything's under control. Oh, send up the doc, will you?"

Edwin Kael came up immediately, picking his way carefully around the puddles of spilled blood. He stooped beside the man who lay with half his back shot away and pressed his index finger against the side of the man's neck. "Just checking," he said. "That's some howitzer you got there, Mister." He was grinning broadly.

In the shifting shadows, Joe began to come around. Kael eased past Dave to look at him.

"Don't get in front of the gun, Doc," said Dave. "Leave him be."

"Couple of nasty wounds. Have to lose both the leg and the arm."

"What now? I get to try and save his life?" He blinked through his broken glasses, seeing the look on the other man's face. He nodded slowly. "No. I guess I don't, do I?"

"No."

Joe tossed his head from side to side, his hair becoming matted in the dribbling stream of blood that was still oozing from the corpse. "Oh, Jesus Christ, Mister! Don't!"

"I'm after Sheever. I know he's a day ahead of me now."

"Day and a half," interrupted Edwin Kael.

"I know he's heading for a box canyon. Around fifty miles from here. Place called Castle Ridge."

"Yeah," said Joe, his voice shriveled suddenly to a whisper.

"He's in shock," said Kael. "Better be quick, or you'll lose him. Lot of blood spent."

"I need to know exactly where he's gone," said Dave, stooping and pressing the muzzle of the Linebaugh into the angle of the small man's jaw, making cartilage crunch.

"You already... said it."

"How will I find the canyon?"

"Cross a lake. Near a big smoldering volcano up... up the valley. Through Castle Ridge. Nobody lives there. Not... not anymore."

Dave hefted the pistol, the polished walnut grip warm against his fingers, and smashed the barrel against the side of Joe's face. The front sight gashed the skin over the narrow cheekbone, bringing a trickle of fresh blood. The man moaned, his head banging back against the wall.

"More," said Dave. "Details."

"I know your daughters are—" began the doctor, standing behind Dave.

"Keep the fuck out of this, will you!"

There was the sound of boots on the stairs behind Dave, and he spun around, his finger whitening on the trigger. When he saw that it was Lee, with Melmoth leashed, and Zera, he pointed for them to stay where they were, at the end of the corridor. Again he turned to the weeping man at his feet.

"Tell me about the canyon."

"Boxed. High cliffs and a pool at far end. No way up or... Oh, Jesus, help me, Mister."

"Did you help those girls?"

"What girls?" There was utter incomprehension in the staring eyes. The tongue flicked out and tasted the threading blood.

"Roxanne and Ellie. Been with you some time now. My daughters!" Dave hit him again with the barrel of the pistol, just above the right eye, the steel ringing off scraped bone.

"Oh, fuck... that was Sheever.... Wouldn't let anyone else..."

Questions clustered at the front of Dave Rand's mind, but he ignored them, not wanting to hear any of those particular answers.

"He's fading," Kael said quietly.

"I don't want him fucking fading. I want him to talk to me."

Joe heaved himself up on his one arm, mouth working. "If those kids was yours, then the woman was your...was your wife. Right?"

"Yeah. But I don't—"

"No...listen. It wasn't me.... The woman was the one that...her and Sheever would..."

Dave jammed the muzzle of the Linebaugh into the mouth of the wounded man. When he pulled the trigger, the kick of the revolver was so powerful that it broke Joe's upper jaw.

"You play some very tough pool," said Edwin Kael. "I'll go get another shot in the bar. You haven't left me much to do up here."

IT WAS ALMOST AN HOUR before father and son had the chance to talk quietly. They'd already agreed they would start after Sheever and his gang at first light.

"Dad. The way you treated those two men..."

"What about it, Lee?"

"Just that I sort of...never knew you had that kind of...had that in you."

Dave sighed. "Nor me. But it's not something that's gotten into me, son. It's something that was inside me all the time. Now it's coming out . . . and it's not for no reason. Just remember who these men were, and what they did to a lot of folks—including your mother.''

9

"There are times when being anywhere else is better than just being somewhere," said Dr. Edwin Kael, pushing his skis across the crisp snow of early morning. "I'm glad the Black Hole is behind me."

Dave hadn't been very enthusiastic about again adding a stranger to what had begun as a personal odyssey. But he had taken an instant liking to the short, skinny black man in the ragged suit, now covered with a dark green anorak.

"It could help the odds against Sheever," Zera had suggested, when the three of them talked it over.

However the argument didn't hold much water when they found that Kael refused point-blank to carry any kind of weapon. But he did agree to wear a horn-handled camper's knife on his belt.

In return for Dave's getting rid of her unwanted guests in room 6, Nancy had told them to take whatever they needed from her well-stocked kitchen. Dave had been delighted to find she had plenty of packets of soup and stews, along with some self-heats, though they were bulky to carry.

The morning was bright when they set off, detouring back to the house where they'd found temporary shelter to pick up the sled. Melmoth was overjoyed to see what he had come to regard as his own special transport and immediately scrambled up on top of it. He perched there, tongue lolling out, looking immensely self-satisfied.

"THERE'S A SMELL of sulfur, coming from the west," said Kael, when they paused for a break.

"Look at the sky over there." Lee had found some ski goggles and pushed them up over his forehead. "Double-menacing."

Dave shaded his eyes with his gloved hand. It was still a couple of hours shy of noon, with the temperature probably a few degrees below freezing. The sun kept breaking through some torn fragments of high, pinkish cloud. The wind was driving from the west, and he realized that he'd been smelling the distinctive sulfur for some time without really being aware of it.

Away to the far west the sky was spectacular. The pale blue shaded into deeper blue, then into purple and finally a funereal black. But behind that were tints of gold and crimson and vermilion. Clouds were rising in towering thunderheads that seemed to topple in on themselves like gigantic aliens that were constantly being reborn and then devouring themselves.

"Some real big volcanic action over there," Dave said. "Looks like it's quite close to where we're heading."

Kael wiped the good lens of his glasses. "Men coming in the Black Hole talked about that."

"What did they say?" asked Zera.

He sniffed. "Think I've got a cold coming. Sorry, lady. What did they say about what?"

"Volcanoes."

"Said there was some bad places—whole valleys filled with rivers of lava, forest burned, towns wiped away by jets of white-hot steam. Mostly in the high country. One man who'd been up near Seattle said the Cascades had become impenetrable."

"Let's move on," Dave spoke up. "Guy back in Altmann said there was a lake to cross."

There was a moment of uncomfortable silence as all of them remembered what had happened to that guy back in Altmann.

THE TRAIL HAD WOUND higher between stands of sick looking timber. Twice they'd been forced to detour where land tilts had shifted waterfalls and sliced across the trail so it ended in a sheer falls of two hundred feet to caverns of whirling spray.

The good thing about following Sheever's mounted party was that they couldn't lose the track. That many horses dug up the rutted, frozen mud, leaving piles of droppings wherever there'd been a halt.

The snow was becoming much sparser, and during the early afternoon they stopped again and took off their skis, binding them across their shoulders. Along with the tent and sleeping bags, the sled loaded with supplies made heavy pulling. Dave regretted not having thought this one through. They could maybe have found some wheels in Altmann or even somewhere along the road and fixed up the sled so it could become a cart.

Now pulling their supplies meant harsh labor.

"Can't go on much longer like this, Dad." Lee panted. "We'll have to leave it and carry what we can."

"Shouldn't be much more than another day or so before we close in on them," said Zera. "Why not travel fast and light?"

It was an appealing suggestion. But Dave's survivalist training dictated hanging on to what they had for as long as possible. Who knew what was waiting around the next bend in the highway or the distant outcrop?

The top of the next hill afforded a view of a series of ridges stretching into the distance, climbing steadily for another two hundred feet. The pine trees grew thicker, holding in the silence around them.

"Let's take a break at the top," Dave said, struggling for breath, feeling as if someone had tightened a steel band around his chest.

"You never said this was going to be serious hard work," Edwin Kael remarked with a grin. "Should have stuck to my job as pox doctor to the rich and famous of Altmann." He paused. "On second thoughts, maybe this *is* better, after all."

"THAT'S THE LAKE," Dave Rand said as he stared ahead, conscious that he was simply stating the obvious.

According to their maps, there wasn't supposed to be a lake for a hundred miles in any direction—never mind one of this stunning grandeur.

"That's a shit lot of water and ice," Zera offered, sitting down on the sled, ignoring Melmoth's protests at being pushed off.

Dave stood and looked down. The cut on his arm was stinging, and he flexed his fingers. Back in Altmann Dr. Kael had offered to stitch the long, shallow wound for him, but Dave had refused the offer. Instead he had asked to have it bandaged tightly.

It was difficult to judge the size of the lake, as its farther end lay beneath a thin veil of mist, but it looked at least five miles across and close to fifteen miles in both directions. The surface was a sullen lead gray, broken up by a network of faint lines. Dave hadn't seen a sizable body of water unfrozen for a year and a half, but the layer of ice on this one looked as if it weren't completely solid.

"Devil of a long way around it, Dave," said Edwin Kael.

"Got to be a good forty to fifty miles if we go at it on foot," he agreed.

"It doesn't look iced right over," Lee commented, holding the lightweight Nikon 9 x 35 glasses, fiddling with the milled knob that controlled the focus. "Some patches seem almost like clear water."

"That's no damned help. It'd be fine if we could walk over. Easy dragging the sled as well. But if it's broken ice, then..." Dave let the sentence trail away.

"How did Sheever and his killers get across?" asked Zera. "Or did they take the long way around?"

They found the answer when they followed the hoof marks down the steep trail toward the water.

"South," Lee whooped. "They've gone the long way around, and the trail looks real difficult."

"Don't sked off like that," Dave warned his son, with the vague feeling that he might have used the slang term incorrectly.

"There's gotta be some way we can get across the lake," replied Lee. "Water's not too frozen. Look at the ripples there."

A half mile from shore there was a sudden movement of the slate-colored water. Slabs of ice broke and tilted, and gushers of spray shot into the air. Even as the four of them watched, the waves came closer toward shore. And they heard a distant rumbling sound.

"Quake!" yelled Dave. "Back from the water's edge, quick."

Even as they moved away, Melmoth barking furiously, they felt the shore start to shiver. The ground rocked, and there was a noise like a subway train rumbling directly beneath their feet. Water lapped, receded, and then surged for the shore.

Zera was slowest, and the icy lake came swilling up over her ankles, sucking at her boots. She cursed as she slithered onward, joining the others finally on the dry shingle.

"Wouldn't want to be out on the lake when something like that happened," she said.

Farther out they could see the result of a smaller aftershock. More ice tilted and thrust upward, surrounded by gray froth and spray. The noise of the earth moving beneath them gradually dulled and faded away.

Finally the lake resumed its placid, leaden appearance. Over on its far side, Dave noticed that the quake had shifted snow from one of the higher peaks in a massive, soundless avalanche.

Edwin Kael took off his spectacles and began to wipe them with a slow, methodical care. "So?" he said. "Around or across?"

"If there was some safe way of getting across, I'd say take that. But I don't see any motorboats waiting to take us on a guided tourist trip."

"There's some kind of jetty sticking out into the lake, about a half mile to the north." Lee passed Dave the binoculars. "See?"

"Yeah. But it looks sort of tumbledown." He handed the glasses on to the young woman. "I guess that's because this lake isn't even on the damned map we got. Maybe someone built it in the past year or so. Let's go take a look."

"Sheever and his men went around the other way," said Zera. "So they maybe didn't even see it."

"Could be," replied Dave.

SOMEONE HAD BUILT a ramshackle hut, set back among the larches, invisible until they got close to it. Lee was running on ahead, but his father called out to him. "Careful!"

The boy slowed, unslinging the scattergun from his shoulders and walking more cautiously toward the partly open door of the hut.

The others ranged out in a half circle, abandoning the cumbersome sled. Dave snapped at the pit bull to keep him at his side, preventing him from rushing on to join Lee.

"Should you allow such a young fellow to take the lead?" asked the doctor. "Not that it's my business, of course."

Dave looked at him. "If I'd thought you were a stupid man, Edwin, I wouldn't have had you along. It *is* your business. Every single thing we do is *your* business. All right?"

"Right, Dave. Loud and very clear."

Lee had pushed at the door with the barrel of the Browning 12-gauge, looked inside and turned away. Then looked again, longer this time.

"Dead woman in here," he called. "Least, I think it's a woman." He moved away, his face pale under the tan. "And there's a sort of a boat as well."

Edwin examined the corpse while the others dragged out the homemade dinghy. Dave had glanced at the body, but it wasn't something that interested him. A part of his mind was fascinated at yet another example of the way his sensibilities had altered since the Big Hit.

"Female, around fifty, been dead somewhere about two months. It's hard to tell how long after the maggots have done their stuff. Likely malnutrition or the cold, pneumonia, maybe frostbite, cholera. Pick what you like, friends. Fact is she's dead."

They found the skeletal remains of a mule in a fenced corral among the trees. Dave guessed the woman must have used the animal to drag timber in from somewhere to build the shelter and the boat.

"This'll never carry us," Zera complained, once they had the craft out on the shore. "Look at the fucker!"

"Looks solid to me," Dave said. "Try floating it and see if it keeps out the lake. That's all that matters. There's two paddles."

"What if it sinks?" Lee asked.

Dave looked at his son. "Frankly, that's a pretty idiotic question, Lee. If it sinks, then we have to struggle all the way around on foot, and lose a lot of time. It floats, and we get there quicker. Close up by a day or more on Sheever. And the girls."

When they tried it out, it leaked a little, but it floated.

10

The stench of sulfur had intensified during the past hour or so, and the sky had already begun to darken. There had been a flurry of hail, pocking the surface of the lake.

"Reckon we should wait until morning to go for it, Dad?" asked Lee as they dragged their supplies from the sled to the boat.

"Yeah. In lots of ways it'd make more sense to do that."

"But . . . ?"

"We're going now."

THE TEMPERATURE was falling faster than a broken elevator. Dave took one of the paddles, heaving at the water that was already scumming over with a thin layer of clear ice. There wasn't much freeboard to the boat, and the little wavelets lapped hungrily at the rough wooden sides, occasionally dribbling in if anyone made a hasty or clumsy movement. Across the lake the mist was thickening.

Melmoth was unhappy at this new, shifting form of transport, and he stood near the bow. At least, that end of the boat wasn't quite as square as the other, so they were assuming it was meant to be the front.

Lee took the other clumsy paddle, knelt and tried to get some sort of rhythm going with his father. But ice was also forming on the round shaft of the short oar, and his hands kept slipping.

"Fuck this," he said. "Can I change sides with you, Dad?"

"No. Best stay where we are. One wrong move, and we're in the water."

"Yeah," Edwin Kael said forcefully. "I have to give you the best advice I can as a man of medicine. If the boat capsizes in the middle of the lake, I see little prospect of any of us surviving. It'd take too long to reach the shore. We'd be dead in about ten minutes is my informed guess."

Zera grinned. "You're a keying pile of laughs, Doc. Pile of laughs."

The mist spread out, enveloping them, and Dave handed the small compass to Zera. In the gloom they had no other way of knowing if they were simply paddling around in circles.

"Christ, it's cold," he said, shivering despite the layers of thermal clothing.

"Paddle keeps hitting thicker ice, Dad," complained Lee. "And you can hear it sort of grinding away under the front of the boat."

"I know. Got to keep moving. Once we get halted we've had it. We'll be frozen in. Ice won't carry our weight, and we'll all freeze to death in the middle of the lake."

Though he said "in the middle," Dave Rand really didn't have much idea how far they'd gone. Assuming it was five miles across, he'd hoped they'd reach the far shore in about an hour and a half. But progress was painfully laborious and slow, and darkness was becoming a real threat.

"We've been going around forty-five minutes," offered Edwin Kael.

"We could be drifting as well. Fair wind from the west, isn't it?"

Dave's paddle jolted against a jagged chunk of ice, and it stopped him from answering Zera. But what the young woman said was absolutely correct. Unable to see any land now, they had no way of knowing how well they were moving, or in what direction.

Melmoth began to whine softly, his eyes darting from Dave to Lee and back again. The fog was starting to freeze into tiny silver crystals all over his short coat, making him look like some ghostly hound from hell.

From the dark wraiths of fog ahead of them, they heard the sudden sound of a rifle shot. Flat, the echoes swallowed by the mist.

Dave and Lee stopped paddling, and the boat lurched clumsily forward. The only sound was water clunking under the bow.

"Can't be anything to do with us," said Edwin Kael. "Nobody could see in this shitty fog."

"It sounded something like an M-16 carbine," said Dave. "Could easily be Sheever."

The shot wasn't repeated, and they started to row cautiously again. But the ice was growing a thicker skin over the lake, harder to break through. And among the sludge of the fresh ice were serious-sized chunks, several feet across, some of them nearly a foot thick.

"If it hadn't been for the quakes breaking up all this, I reckon we could have taken a chance on crossing it on foot," Dave said, then paused to take several long panting breaths.

Lee was also resting, doubled over, head on his chest. The paddle was trailing over the side. Dave warned him to take care with it.

"I'm fucked, Dad. Sorry, but . . ."

"Let me," Zera volunteered.

"Better let me have a turn. You can spell Dave when he needs a rest."

The young woman looked steadily across at the short, slim black man who had spoken. With infinite courtesy she held out her right hand to him and threw him a finger. "Me," she said.

Dave glanced down at his watch. "If my calculations are right, we should be getting close to shore. This boat's so unsteady it could tip if we change places."

"Just give me the paddle. I can work it from here," insisted Zera.

"And I'll try the other one," Edwin offered. "I'm freezing and some work would help. Will help. Pass it, Dave."

They moved a little faster for five minutes or so, then Edwin lost his paddle over the side. It had jarred against a monster floe, at least fifty feet in width, and had been whipped from his chilled fingers. He made a desperate grab for it as it dropped onto the gray, rippled ice, but the boat moved on and the fog closed around it.

"Fuck, bastard, asshole, fuck, fuck, fuck!"

The brief litany was delivered in a calm, gentle voice, as though he were reading aloud to himself from a motel breakfast menu.

"Can't be helped," Dave said, fighting down a sudden blazing anger at the other man's clumsiness. Now their progress would be even more difficult to control, with only the compass to hold them to an approximate course. With just a single paddle they would inevitably start to pitch to one side.

The prow clipped sharply against another big floe and lurched to starboard, immediately striking more thick ice and coming to a halt. Turgid water slopped over the side as Melmoth jumped into Lee's lap.

Then rain began to fall, mixed with large flakes of wet snow.

Dave made an attempt to break up some of the ice that now blocked their progress across the lake. It was as futile, he thought, as trying to pick the lock on a pay-toilet door with a piece of wet string.

Though they knew they were afloat somewhere in the middle of a huge lake, the boat was motionless, gripped by the clamping vise of the thickening ice field. The fog lay around them like a shroud, soaking them through their layers of clothing. The snow continued to fall inexorably.

Dave sucked in cold air through his teeth, making a face as it touched where a filling was missing in a back tooth. It was only really late afternoon, but night was swamping them and there could be at least twelve hours to go before daylight approached. If they were still trapped on the lake by then, it was an even bet that they wouldn't all be alive.

"Take a chance on walking?" asked Zera, then shook her head. "Sorry. Stupid. 'Course not."

Dave stood, taking great care to maintain his balance. He peered all around in the desperate hope that he might somehow be able to see above the clinging bank of fog.

But there was nothing.

"What's that?" Lee asked, cocking his head.

"What?"

"Listen. Kind of a creaking..."

"Groaning noise," Zera finished for him. "Yeah." She laid her hand on the thwart of the makeshift craft. "It's vibrating, Dave."

There was still some vaporous residual light, and Dave peered over the side onto the surface of the lake.

"Fuck it," he said quietly. "The ice is thickening so fast it's starting to clamp on the boat. Crushing the side."

"It's already sprung a plank down here by my feet, Captain Rand," Edwin said.

"All hands to the pumps. Maybe Melmoth feels real thirsty." Lee tried for the joke, but the tremor in his voice betrayed him.

"Sure the ice won't take our weight, Dave?" asked Zera.

"In another few minutes we're going to find out," he replied.

THEY WERE BUSY MINUTES.

Dave knew that Edwin's earlier words were true: once the boat broke up and they were in the lake, it would be only a handful of freezing moments before their circulation slowed and one by one they slipped under the gray water.

"Leave the tent," he ordered. "Leave anything heavy except for the guns and the ammo."

"Sleeping bags?"

"No."

"Food?"

Dave shook his head. "No point. If we make it, we'll have to hunt."

"Water?" asked Edwin, managing a wry smile.

"Sure. We could be real short of that about ten minutes from now."

The boat's timbers were groaning loudly under the growing strain from the crushing ice, and water was seeping into the bottom through a dozen widening cracks. Melmoth was in Lee's arms, silent and cowed by the immensity of the fog around them.

"Should we take off our boots?" Zera asked. "We might swim better without them."

"No. Make it with them or not at all. Reach land barefoot, and it won't be long before your toes start rotting away."

"Big crack opening here," Edwin commented, calm as ever.

"Listen. There's that rumbling like when—"

Lee didn't get to finish the sentence. The roaring noise grew louder, like a runaway diesel semi coming at them from the blinding mist. The ice fragmented with the sound of a thousand pistol shots. The boat lurched sideways and then dipped under the water.

It didn't precisely sink.

One moment it was still above the surface of the frozen lake. A nanosecond later and it was gone.

DAVE RAND GASPED IN a great gulp of cold foggy air before he was sucked under.

He tried to push off, but the boat went under too quickly and he was immediately floundering in pitch-blackness. His clothes kept off the immediate shock of the biting chill, but his face was instantly numbed. The rifle and machine pistol across his shoulders tugged him backward at an awkward angle, and he kicked and flailed for life.

The water seemed fillcd with sharp ice, and he wasn't able to find any purchase to swim to the surface. The air in his lungs was shrinking, and his head was still underwater. The utter blackness was so disorienting that Dave didn't know which way was up.

A hand grabbed at his belt and then slipped away again from him.

His feet jarred against a particularly large chunk of thick ice and he found a momentary foothold and pushed himself away from it.

There was the blessed surge of fresh air around him, and he drew a long, whooping breath, crouched in the water, feet still against the ice.

It took him a dozen heartbeats to become aware of where he was and what was happening.

It wasn't ice.

He was doubled up, with the soles of his boots resting on the bottom of the lake. Almost kneeling in less than four feet of icy water!

"Here!" he yelled, voice cracking. "Over here! Land here!"

Moments later Lee and Zera came splashing toward him through the shallows. They hugged one another, then stopped, staring out into the grayness, looking for Edwin and Melmoth.

Land and water and sky were blurred into a leaden mass.

Apart from the delicate lapping of the wavelets around their feet, it was deathly silent.

11

"I'll go back in," Zera offered.

"No."

"I'll be fine."

She was shaken by violent paroxysms, and her teeth were chattering hard enough to break.

"We got three alive. Let's keep it that way," said Dave. "Now shut up and listen."

"Something out there," Lee said, grabbing at his father's elbow.

"Shut up!"

Then they heard it—three separate sounds, all melding together. A hollow banging, Melmoth barking excitedly and someone yelling for help.

"Edwin," they said, more or less at the same moment.

"Help! I'm drowning...." The voice shut off as though a switch had been thrown somewhere out in the fog.

"He must be just beyond the shallows," Dave said. "Edwin! Over here!"

The only sound now was a splashing and panting. And the whisper of a freshening wind, taking away the remnants of the snow.

Lee pointed at the lake excitedly. "There! Hey...Melmoth's gotten him out safe."

His hair silvered with fresh ice, glasses hooked over his left ear, Dr. Edwin Kael of Seattle had all the natural dignity of a drowned marmot. The pit bull had his teeth locked into the shoulder of the man's suit, swimming along bravely, head held high.

"It's only two feet deep, Doc!" bellowed the young woman. "Put your fucking boots down and walk!"

"Is that the voice of Our Savior...or is it that Zera person?" gasped Dr. Kael, but he took her advice and struggled erect, water streaming from his clothes.

Surrounded by the shifting banks of mist, he looked like some looming monster from an ancient horror vid. Melmoth pattered ashore, shook himself, then paraded proudly up and down, collecting pats and praise from everyone.

"I'll never say another word against that four-legged death machine," said Edwin, joining the shuddering trio on the shingle beach.

1. How do you rate: _____

(Please print book TITLE)

AA1234

- 1.6 ☐ Excellent
- .5 ☐ Very good
- .4 ☐ Good
- .3 ☐ Fair
- .2 ☐ Not so good
- .1 ☐ Poor

2. How likely are you to purchase another book:

In this *series*?

- 2.1 ☐ Definitely would purchase
- .2 ☐ Probably would purchase
- .3 ☐ Probably would not purchase
- .4 ☐ Definitely would not purchase

By this *author*?

- 3.1 ☐ Definitely would purchase
- .2 ☐ Probably would purchase
- .3 ☐ Probably would not purchase
- .4 ☐ Definitely would not purchase

3. How does this book compare with the action books you usually read?

- 4.1 ☐ Far better than others
- .2 ☐ Better than others
- .3 ☐ About the same
- .4 ☐ Not as good
- .5 ☐ Definitely not as good

4. What most prompted you to buy this book?

- 5. ☐ Read other books in series
- 6. ☐ In-store display
- 7. ☐ Cover illustration
- 8. ☐ Title
- 9. ☐ Author
- 10. ☐ Advertising
- 11. ☐ Story outline on back
- 12. ☐ Ad inside other book
- 13. ☐ Friend's recommendation

5. Which of the following other Gold Eagle action series have you read?

- 14. ☐ Executioner/ Mack Bolan
- 15. ☐ Stoney Man
- 16. ☐ Agents
- 17. ☐ Soldiers of War
- 18. ☐ Survival 2000
- 19. ☐ Deathlands
- 20. ☐ Horn
- 21. ☐ Time Warriors
- 22. ☐ Phoenix Force
- 23. ☐ Able Team
- 24. ☐ Vietnam: Ground Zero
- 25. ☐ Barrabas/SOBs

6. Which of the following categories of action fiction would you like to see more new series from or about?

- 26. ☐ Urban crime wars
- 27. ☐ Anti-drug wars
- 28. ☐ Espionage
- 29. ☐ Western
- 30. ☐ Science fiction
- 31. ☐ Horror/occult
- 32. ☐ Other: _____
- 33. ☐ Future crime wars
- 34. ☐ Post-holocaust
- 35. ☐ Future war
- 36. ☐ Anti-terrorist
- 37. ☐ Martial arts
- 38. ☐ High-tech crime
- 39. ☐ WW II combat
- 40. ☐ Vietnam combat
- 41. ☐ Paramilitary
- 42. ☐ Future techno-thriller
- 43. ☐ High adventure
- 44. ☐ Police drama

7. Where did you obtain this book?

- 45. ☐ Bookstore
- 46. ☐ Drugstore
- 47. ☐ Supermarket
- 48. ☐ Military store
- 49. ☐ Department/ discount store
- 50. ☐ Convenience store
- 51. ☐ Borrowed
- 52. ☐ Used
- 53. ☐ Other: _____

8. Please indicate how many action fiction paperbacks you buy in a month?

- 54.1 ☐ 1 or 2
- .2 ☐ 3 or 4
- .3 ☐ 5 to 10
- .4 ☐ More than 10

9. Please indicate your sex and age group:

- 55.1 ☐ Male
- .2 ☐ Female
- 56.1 ☐ Under 18
- .2 ☐ 18 to 24
- .3 ☐ 25 to 34
- .4 ☐ 35 to 49
- .5 ☐ 50 to 64
- .6 ☐ 65 or older

Gold Eagle thanks you for sharing your opinions and returning this survey!

(57 – 61) ☐☐☐☐☐

Printed in Canada

NAME _____
(Please Print)

ADDRESS _____

CITY _____

ZIP CODE _____

BUSINESS REPLY MAIL

FIRST CLASS   PERMIT NO. 717   BUFFALO, NY

POSTAGE WILL BE PAID BY ADDRESSEE

NATIONAL READER SURVEYS

P.O. Box 1395
Buffalo, N.Y. 14240-9961

"You won't have a chance to say anything un-less we get some kind of heat to dry ourselves out," said Dave. "Wet and cold are two of the biggest killers. I've got some matches in my waterproof pack. Everyone get going and find some wood. Should be plenty of dead stuff on the fringes of those trees." He indicated the stark outlines of tall pines that poked through the dark fog.

THE FIRE WAS immensely satisfying. Lee had been particularly industrious, staggering along under a mountain of bone-dry, brittle wood that he'd scav-enged from the edge of the forest. They'd got the fire going with some small twigs and bits of bark, built into a careful pyramid by Dave Rand and lit with a single, valuable match. The flickering yel-low flame was guarded against the rising breeze until it gathered strength. Then it was fed and fed again as it eagerly devoured everything put before it.

At Dave's orders they stripped out of their wet clothes and hung them on forked branches stuck deep into the beach, where they steamed and writhed in the ferocious glow of the fire. Boots were ranged in a neat line a few feet away to avoid dam-aging the leather, and the guns and other equip-ment were stacked at a safe distance.

The center of the blaze was a shimmering white inferno, painful to look at. Surrounding it was a core of yellow-orange, gradually fading away to crimson. The branches cracked and popped, exploding into white ash, making it hazardous to sit too close to them.

The men wore only underpants, while Zera huddled in bikini pants and a fluorescent T-shirt. She never wore a bra.

"Think we're on the right side of the lake, Dave?" Zera asked.

"Should be. Compass bearing was steady, and we kept moving until the ice stopped us. Still, we'll know in the morning."

"Wonder if Sheever is anywhere near us?" Lee said. "If we've saved as much time as we hope, we could be double-close to him by now."

"If he's near, then he'll see this fire if the fog lifts." Dave grinned. "In fact, if the fog lifts, they could probably see our bonfire as far away as Schenectady."

Edwin Kael looked at him curiously. "Why Schenectady?"

Dave shrugged. "Why not?"

"What's the time, Dad?" asked Lee. "Must be around midnight."

"Nearly one. How's everyone feeling? Edwin?"

"Still trying to get over the fact that I feel like someone who's just had the 'most unforgettable event of his life.' If there were any magazines still being printed, then I could make Melmoth a national hero."

"Yeah. But how do you *feel?*"

"Considering I've been frozen and nearly drowned in the past few hours, I'm in great shape."

"Fog's clearing, Dad."

It was gradually rolling away from them, off the land, drifting back across the icebound water of the lake.

Dave turned to face Zera. "How are *you* feeling? Warm enough?"

She smiled at him, pushing back the jagged blond fringe of hair from over her blue eyes. "I'm ready to kick some ass, Dave. If the fire gets any hotter, I'll start to turn into barbecued steak."

Dave smiled. For a moment a thought came whispering into his mind that he was falling in love with the young woman who was barely older than his daughter Ellie, and much, much younger than himself.

He pulled his eyes away from her lean, muscular body, patched with flickering shadows from the bonfire, and pushed the unbidden thought back from the center of his mind.

"Lee? You look okay to me. About time you had a good wash, anyway."

"Thanks, Dad. You're a prince among men. And I have to tell you that your armpits were no longer charmpits, either."

"We got off lightly. Lost the tent and some other stuff. At least we had a few minutes' warning to get ourselves organized."

"We'll need some food soon," Edwin remarked.

"Got all the weapons we'll need." The guns were safe, drying out by the blazing branches. The bows and arrows had also made it through.

"Hey, the fog's almost completely gone," said Lee, standing up, ribs etched stark by the firelight. "And there's a moon coming through."

Dave also got to his feet and slowly turned in a circle, seeing the edge of the forest, impenetrably dark and threatening. The mountain loomed over them, and he could now make out the far side of the lake. The sliver of bright moon hung between banks of high cloud, casting its light off the dull ice on the water.

Since Adastreia's impact with Earth, the weather changes were much faster and much less predictable than they used to be.

Melmoth pattered down to the edge of the lake and lapped at the ice-free fringe. He turned suddenly, head ranging from side to side as though he had heard or seen something but couldn't quite locate it.

"What is it, boy?" said Dave.

All of a sudden he was frighteningly aware of their near-nakedness and visibility. They were exposed on a spur of land, with water in front of them and the trees and the hills behind them, standing by a blazing fire that must be like a beacon for miles.

Sheever and his gang had to be somewhere in the neighborhood, possibly within a few miles of them at that moment. But maybe even closer.

He started toward his clothes, mouth dry, heart beginning to pound. "Come on," he said tersely. "Let's—"

The burst of bullets cut short his words.

THE HALO OF LIGHT from the bonfire made it almost impossible to discern any details beyond it. The shots came from the hillside somewhere above them, definitely from their side of the lake.

"Two or three," said Lee, lying flat on his face just inside the edges of the trees. "I think only two."

That was Dave's own guess. Both of their attackers were using automatic rifles, and they were probably quite high up. Static, brightly illuminated by the burning wood, he and the other three should have been sitting targets for any reasonable marksmen. But he knew himself that the most difficult shot was downhill, at a distance.

He was pleased at the way everyone had reacted to the shooting. They had grabbed for clothes and weapons, except for Dr. Kael who'd gone for clothes and Melmoth, scooping up the pit bull under his arm as he scampered for cover.

He and Zera were a few yards along the top of the beach from Dave and Lee. After the first blast of shooting, with bullets zipping and howling off the stones across the lake, the firing had become much more sporadic.

"Reckon it's Sheever?" Lee asked.

Dave Rand had been asking himself precisely the same question. He came up with the answer—deeply unsatisfying to his exacting nature—that it *probably* was Sheever—or a couple of his men.

"Scouts or rear guard?" he muttered to himself, hoping it was the latter. It was better by far to be still safe on the trail of the gang, rather than somehow trapped between parts of the group.

A triple salvo of bullets hissed into the treetops above them, bringing a shower of pine needles into their hair. While undercover, they'd all struggled into clothes to keep warm away from the fire.

"If that would die down we could move safely," said Dave. "It can't burn forever."

"Why not shoot back?" Lee whispered. "You got the Leupold optical sight on the Lux rifle. It's worth a couple of shots."

"No."

"No?"

Dave explained his thinking. "They can't know—not actually *know*—that we're after them. Sheever's probably got guys out front and back to keep his ass safe, warn off anyone gets close. We know what happens to poor bastards who actually fall into his hands. So, they see the fire and spot us by it. Put a few rounds in our direction."

"I get it! We start shooting at them, and they'll take us double-serious! We lie quiet, and they'll probably fuck off and leave us alone."

"That's the idea, son."

"And we chase them."

"Have to move fast and carefully now. They've got horses but the terrain's hard. From the smell and the sky, it seems like there's some serious volcanic activity up ahead of us."

Another round of bullets made everyone duck.

But it was the last of the shooting.

Well before dawn the fire finally died away, leaving a pile of soft gray ash. Dawn came up over the lake, now frozen over completely, shore to shore.

By then Dave and his group were already a third of the way up the mountain, climbing with a careful purpose.

Closing in on Sheever and his men.

And the two lonely, frightened girls.

12

The next day and a half were cold and dismal. The hills seemed stripped clear of game. Since they knew they were close to their prey, it would have been suicidal to use firearms. They saw an occasional woodchuck and a couple of rabbits, but it proved too late by the time they had the bow strung and an arrow notched to the string.

"My stomach and spine have never been so well acquainted," Edwin Kael remarked, trying to stretch the aches away.

They'd stopped for a short break just after noon. At least, their watches told them it was the middle of the day, but the sun's face was veiled behind dense clouds of blackish gray.

Zera lay on her back on the soft pine needles at the side of the track and stared up at where the sun should have been. "The sun will not be seen today...." she said. "A thing devised by the enemy."

"That's *Richard III*," Dave said. "Yeah, good old Shakespeare."

"I majored in Sports Meditation. My minor was Eng. Lit. I'm not just a pretty face, Dave."

"I know," he said, hiding his embarrassment behind a broad smile.

Last night, bundled together under some dry brush, Zera had cried out as she climaxed beneath him, so loudly that she had wakened both Lee and Edwin.

Dave had tried to talk to her about it, falling back to walk alongside her. But the young woman had only grinned at him.

"Hey, Dave, we're back to nature here, or what's left of it. So why make a problem of it? We either do it or not do it."

"It's just that I don't know what's coming."

"Then just let things be...."

There was no need for Zera to say anything more. They both knew that the as-yet-unseen reality would make choices for them ... and they might be choices they wouldn't want themselves.

WITH EVERY HOUR that passed, Dave was becoming more and more concerned. It was clear from the tracks that they were certainly keeping up with Sheever and his party, maybe even closing a little.

But the going was heartbreakingly hard.

The map was useless to them. Apart from the fact that the large lake was not even shown on it, the mountains seemed to have been rearranged, forming new trails and rivers and valleys. They passed through a whole region where earth movements had brought down a forest and scattered trees two hundred feet tall in a shapeless tangle of dead and dying wood.

Nature had wrought a crazed landscape, but Nature was also working at restoring some kind of order from the chaos. Small animals, and then bigger creatures, had started to move through the land, creating narrow, twisting paths that speedily grew wider. Several times during the tiring climb Lee spotted mountain goats, with curly horns, picking their way along invisible trails far above. They were within range of the Sauer rifle, but it would have taken the better part of a day to try and retrieve the carcass.

Hunger began to haunt them, a lean and skeletal figure in a ragged cloak and with crook'd fingernails. Its beckoning shadow was ahead of them, behind them, all around them.

The days were bright and cool, and the nights starlit and freezing. They broke trail in turns, leading for an hour at a time, then taking up the rear position. Always changing and always moving higher.

And Dave grew ever more worried.

When they stopped to eat a handful of berries that Zera had spotted in some tangled undergrowth, Dave sat alone. He scooped up a handful of snow from a shaded hollow and sucked at it to quench his thirst.

Edwin Kael walked over to join him. "I do beg your pardon, but is this table reserved?"

Dave laughed. "Looks like my dinner date is a no-show. Do sit down."

Edwin hunkered down alongside him, leaning against the bole of a dead live oak. He had a long scratch on his cheek from a lashing bramble.

"How's that knife cut?"

"Healing."

"Sure?"

"Sure."

"No thin red lines weaving up the inside of your arm and hideous swellings of black and scarlet in your armpit?"

"Oh, those? Yeah I got those, Doc, but I always have them."

"Take a couple of painkillers and make an appointment with my secretary in the morning. No, wait a moment, tomorrow's Thursday. I'll be on the golf course. Better make it Friday."

Dave laughed again. "Is it really Thursday tomorrow, Doc?"

"Who the fuck knows days anymore? I don't."

They sat silent for a minute or two, listening to the faint sounds of the woods around them. Edwin broke the silence. "What's up, Dave?"

"I thought the line was: 'What's up, Doc?' Like in the kids' Saturday cartoons."

"I'm not joking now, Dave."

"Hell, I knew that. It's the way we're getting real close to Sheever."

"That's what we're here for, isn't it?"

"Sure."

"So?"

"We have to reckon that this bastard's got some kind of strength and organization. Right?" Kael nodded his agreement. "They saw the fire night before last and they tried to gun us down. But they didn't try very hard."

"So, you think he might worry about it? Maybe have it nagging at him so he eventually sends someone back to find out if there might, just possibly, be someone following him?"

"Right. A trail like this could have two guys with LMGs around any corner."

"Nothing much we can do."

Dave stood up and stretched. "Not a lot. Just be real careful."

After their short respite they moved on, and by evening they'd reached the crest of the hill and were able to camp in the open.

There was a return of the fog that had lain across the lake like a blight. Now it filled the valley stretching before them, so that it resembled a shifting bowl of steaming soup.

"You think Sheever's still heading for that box canyon place?" asked Zera.

"Must be. But the map's totally fucked. The way we thought he'd go just doesn't exist anymore. That's why we're going this way."

Lee was kneeling and patting Melmoth. The dog was increasingly affected by the lack of food and was no longer keen to scamper ahead of them but contented himself with dragging at their heels.

"We heard that rifle shot only an hour or so back. Probably means they're hunting. From what we've seen at their campsites, they don't have a lot of tinned or packaged food left." The boy straightened. "Maybe that place, Castle Ridge, is down the valley there. Could mean food."

"Or it could mean Sheever," said Dave.

THE NIGHT WAS QUIET.

Over the past eighteen months, Dave had gotten used to sleeping out in the open on the ground. He automatically kept on his clothes, including the hood of his parka, retaining body heat for as long as possible. He curled up, hands between thighs, keeping very close to the others. They took comfort and warmth from one another's nearness.

He woke around five in the morning, rubbing his hand over his chin, feeling the particles of ice clustered in the stubble of his growing beard. Moving carefully to avoid disturbing Lee, Zera and Edwin, he stood up and took a leak a few yards away, on the edge of the valley. Melmoth came over and stood by him, as though he was scared of missing out on some secret midnight snack.

"Nothing to eat, boy." He stooped to rub his fingers through the stiff, prickling hairs across the pit bull's powerful shoulders. "Have to try and shoot some game tomorrow—unless there's something down there under all that fog."

The dog pressed his flank against Dave's leg, seeking reassurance. Dave patted him again, then stood up, hand against the cold bark of the tree. His eyes drifted over the top of the mist, watching how its rounded whiteness undulated, seemed to rise and fall. And fall again.

"What . . . ?" he said wonderingly.

As the fog sank and dissipated across the valley, it began to reveal a strange sight. The tops of a tented city began to appear. Most of the tents were makeshift, patched efforts, resembling Indian te-pees. Indeed, for one mind-shifting moment Dave Rand thought that he'd somehow time-slipped and was on the Washita overlooking the last great gathering of the Sioux nations.

At a quick count there were at least eighty to a hundred tents in the shallow valley, with the gleam of a river coursing through it. There was also the ruby sparkle of many smoldering camp fires scattered over the basin.

The moon showed the ruins of a strange complex of buildings, way above the tented city. At a distance it wasn't possible to make out what those buildings had once been, and Dave resolved to examine the site more carefully through the glasses once dawn came.

On his way back to wriggle among the others and snatch another hour or so of sleep, Dave jumped aside as something jittered across his path. Melmoth growled menacingly and went toward it.

"Leave it, boy," Dave warned. "Could be something poisonous."

He stepped closer, making a face when he saw that the creature was a cockroach. But it was the biggest one he'd ever seen. It was fully seven inches long, with weirdly elongated antennae equipped with tiny hooks all along them. Its body was an iridescent green, and it gave the illusion of actually glowing in the moonlight.

Dave stamped on it, expecting to feel a fragile crackling as it disintegrated beneath the ridged sole of his boot. But there was nothing. The roach had scuttled away from him with surprising speed.

"You little fuck," he muttered, watching the creature as it stopped, its head turning toward him.

He feinted at it, seeing it move to the left, away from the threat. But he was quicker, hitting it hard and feeling an extraordinary resistance, as if the carapace were armor-plated. Then it cracked, and he caught a dreadful stench of putrefaction from its split body.

Melmoth had come closer to investigate but retreated quickly, shaking his head from side to side as if someone had sprayed pepper in his eyes.

"Pretty hideous, huh? Well that's one roach that's finally checked into insect heaven. And won't be checking out again."

He got back to sleep, and when real morning came, he was the last to wake, finding the others lined up along the ridge, staring down into the spread city of quilted tents below.

"Hi, Dad. Come look at this."

"Saw it last night. I got up for a leak just as the fog was moving away."

"We might find food down there," Zera suggested.

"What do we have to trade for it?"

"Me," she replied unhesitatingly, looking round in the startled stillness at the faces of the three men.

"No," Dave said, his voice flat as earth on a coffin lid.

"You have a better idea, old-timer? How about one of you spreading it down there? No? Then don't get all picky about me doing it."

"Cross that bridge when we come to it. I'm not going to be stupid about this. 'Course we need food, and we don't have much to trade. But there could be work. Ordinary work for all of us."

"I'd best stay up here. Or come down just to the edge of that tent town."

They all looked at Edwin Kael. Lee saw the answer first. "Sheever knows you from Altmann. He sees you again, he'll know it's some sort of chase."

Edwin nodded. "Not many guys up these parts look like me or even dress like me. It's safer if I stay out of sight."

Dave considered. "If Sheever and his men are there, then any confrontation has to be on our terms. Any other way and we lose. Lose big and final. Raggedy place like this doesn't look too threatening."

"Lots of tents," Zera said doubtfully.

"We walk carefully, and we're carrying some very big sticks. Any trouble and we're shooting and away from there."

"Sounds right," agreed Lee. "Do we go in together or one at a time?"

"Together," Dave said firmly. "Come partway with us, Edwin, and then we'll find a safehouse or something for you to hide in."

In short order they set off down the trail, muddy and deep-rutted by what looked like wagon wheels. Melmoth was becoming more like his old self—running ahead, bristling with self-importance, cocking a leg at anything he considered worth marking.

"He can smell that bacon cooking down there," Lee said with a grin.

Dave's eye was caught by the large ruins that dominated the valley and remembered he hadn't checked them out with the glasses.

"Ruins are just ruins," he said to himself.

13

It was clear that the area had been appallingly ravaged by some disaster, linked to the Big One. There were enough derelict houses around to show that a town had once stood here. It might even have been Castle Ridge. A map and the land no longer seemed to have any logical relationship, one to another.

Every one of the buildings of the township had been wrecked. From the evidence of the splintered windows and crazy roofs, Dave guessed some enormous blast must have occurred.

The other thing he noticed was the number and size of the insects and vermin. Cockroaches were everywhere, trudging across the road, seeming oblivious to either the cold or the proximity of humans. And Lee spotted a rat darting around that he swore was bigger than a cat.

In the end, Dave had decided it would be better to leave Melmoth with Edwin. If trouble came suddenly from a clear sky, they'd need to move out quickly, and speed wasn't the strongest point of the pit bull's armory.

Zera walked beside Dave, Lee a few paces ahead of them.

"You decided yet?" she asked quietly, eyes searching his face.

"What?" He pretended ignorance, but knew what she meant.

"You know."

"Let's wait and see."

"Dave, if we need food and I can earn it, then it doesn't matter. I lent you my knife the other day."

"So?"

"That belongs to me and so does my body. I don't see the difference."

"Well, I do." He stopped, then waved for Lee to keep going ahead of them. "Listen, I'm not saying you shouldn't. Just that I don't want you to . . . do that. But if it's really the only way . . . All these tomorrows bring new problems."

"Tomorrow's just a different version of today, Dave. We're getting through this one, and we'll get through the next one."

He touched her shoulder briefly to move her on, not looking her in the face.

They reached the first of the outlying tents, which were noticeably more ragged than those nearer the center that they'd seen from the hillside above.

"Jesus!" exclaimed Lee. "The town sewer isn't working very well. And these bastard flies..." He batted at the cloud of huge insects that had appeared from nowhere to surround them.

The smell was truly horrific, a cloacal stench that seemed to rise from the tents in a miasmic haze of revolting pestilence, gripping them by the throat. Dave gasped and shook his head, feeling himself gagging, about to throw up.

"That's the...I can't go on into this."

An old man was watching them from the nearest tent. He sat in the dirt, whittling away at a piece of twisted wood. "You gets used to it, friends," he cackled. "Me, I don't not notice it no more."

He was wearing blue overalls, and his face was in shadow. His legs were stretched out in front of him, and there was a plate and mug at his side.

"This Castle Ridge?" asked Dave.

"Might've been and might've not been. Tell you one thing, friends...."

"What?"

"If it might've been Castle Ridge once, it sure ain't Castle Ridge no more."

"You live here, Mister?" asked Dave.

"Here's like everywhere. I like a place where nothing happens. And that's here."

Zera shook her head. "Wrong, Mister. Nothing happens every place."

"That's a good one, lady. Hey, was you ever bit by a dead roach?"

"He's mad," said Lee. "Let's go in and try to get something to eat."

"You think I'm mad in the head, son? Go on in and see if you find some that are real double-mad. Crazier than shithouse rats, most of them."

"Any chance of food?" asked Dave. He found to his surprise that the old man was right. After a few minutes he did start to get used to the smell.

"You got something to sell?" He leered at Zera in a way that made Dave want to push his face out the back of his narrow skull.

"Maybe," she replied. "But you don't look to me like a man with anything to offer."

He shuffled out on his backside into the watery morning sunlight. He could have been anywhere between thirty-five and seventy. His hair was almost gone, and his scalp and face were covered in peeling sores, particularly thickly crusted around his eyes and lips.

"I got some oatmeal and a can of beans. Trade them for an hour with the lady."

"Not this time, thanks," Zera said, turning to Dave. "Right now you might be right. Let's go farther in and ask some more."

Lee stepped closer. "You seen a real tall guy with triple-blond hair? Gang of men on horses and a couple of girls with them?"

"Sure. Left noon yesterday. Pretty little girls, they was."

Dave walked quickly away, ignoring the rest of the old man's words, blanking his mind to them. Zera and Lee caught up with him, but he gave them both a look that shut their mouths.

As they wandered through the maze of lanes and alleys among the tents, nearly everyone looked to be ill. They passed at least a half dozen corpses, two of them children; most looked as if they'd been lying rotting in the open for days. Several of the bodies seemed to have had slices of flesh cut away from the arms and legs.

But the living didn't look much better than the dead.

"I've never seen so many sick people in my life," said Zera.

Everyone seemed to have lost hair, and many had scabs and sores on their faces and arms. Most sat around lethargically. One young woman sitting behind a caldron of nameless, noisome stew, tried to attract the visitors' attention.

"Good food, strangers. Trade you for a bowl each of this good food."

"What do you want for a bowl each?"

"Them boots look—" She stopped and probed into her mouth with dirty fingers, then pulled out the bleeding stump of a back tooth. "Third this week," she stated with a grin.

"I'll pass on the stew," said Dave. "Got anything else to eat?"

She looked up at him. "You look well, Mister. Real healthy. How d'you feel about selling me some loving comfort for an hour or so? I got some dried meat and a few self-heat cans. Could talk a deal inside."

He looked at her wordlessly. She was around the middle twenties, but was pale and drawn. Blood was trickling from her lips. She wore a pair of cream trousers, and Dave noticed that the crotch was heavily stained with what might have been old blood.

Zera cast a quick glance around. Nobody else was taking any notice of them. She knelt in the opening to the tent and reached inside her anorak, drew the polished Ruger and jammed the muzzle under the woman's throat.

"How about this for a fucking trade," she said softly. "I don't blow your head off, and you give us some food? Deal?"

The woman looked back at her, seeming unworried by the threat of the gun. "Be doing me a favor, child," she said gently.

"What?"

"Castle Ridge? Castle Cemetery more like. Since the place on the hill got blown out in the big quake it's been—" A coughing fit took her breath. "Gets worse each day. First few months it . . . Listen, you need food that bad, then you take it. I won't stop you, girlie. There's some bread, milk I traded for at the farm tent, jerky. Take it."

The woman kept her word, allowing them to take what they wanted from her poor stock. Dave helped himself only to what they immediately needed. The milk was welcome, and the bread, the strips of dried meat and six self-heats without labels.

She watched them, noticing with a grim smile that they were taking only a part of her store. "Real kind of you all," she said. "Means I can keep going for one more week instead of two."

"There must be game around," said Dave.

"Not for miles. Not after the place on the hill did its stuff. But there's no where to go and no way to get there."

"What was the big ruin?" asked Lee.

"Place on the hill."

"But *what* was it?"

"What it always was, son. It was the sun and the moon and gold and silver to us who lived around Castle Ridge."

"And now?" Zera asked gently.

"Now, girlie? It's what you see and hear . . . and smell. That's all."

"Better go," urged Lee. "Edwin'll be getting worried if we're gone too long."

"Sure you can't spare me one of them pretty little bullets from your shiny pistol, child?"

Zera shook her head, close to tears.

"I understand. Still, you left me plenty. All my amphetamines and my pearls and lots and lots of lovely fog."

They left her, not saying much. Some frail children threw a flurry of stones at them as they made their way back through the tented settlement toward the hillside and the open country beyond.

"Little bastards," said Lee, rubbing his thigh where one of the pebbles had hit him.

"Smell of sulfur is back," Zera noticed. "Being down there the shit swamped every other smell in the universe."

"A storm's on the way as well," Dave agreed. "Let's push on into the trees."

"What about moving after Sheever?" Lee was leading them and he looked over his shoulder at his father.

"We'll eat first and then come down again, detour around that place."

"Just the bread and milk'll do me," Lee said eagerly.

"Me, too," Zera said. "My mouth gets all wet and excited at the idea. Know what I mean, Dave?" She licked her lips and smiled.

As far as he was able, the man ignored her. But it wasn't easy.

It was all Edwin could do to restrain Melmoth when the pit bull recognized the sound of Dave's and Lee's feet on the rough track outside.

"What was it like?" he asked.

"Death City, U.S.A.," said Lee. "Triple-grim. There was..."

His father interrupted him. "Talk after, Lee. I think Zera's right. We should move on while we can. Sheever's only a half day or so ahead of us,

Edwin. We'll take the food and milk and push on fast and hard until dusk. Then we can relax and really enjoy what we've got."

ON THE WAY to the east of the tent town they walked along the edge of a dry gulch. Old snow, smeared with dirt, lay in the hollows, packed under the banks. A mere trickle of water could be seen among the rubbish that filled the riverbed.

"Lot of dead fish," said Edwin. "It looks like there was some kind of chemical spillage."

Dave paused, pointing above and behind them to where the jagged ruins of concrete cliffs and twisted metal still dominated the valley. "Place on the hill," he said.

THEY CAMPED as dusk was settling down. The threatened storm had skirted them to the south. Fog had once again brimmed into the bowl at their backs, and they'd climbed up and over a ridge and found a good place to stop among trees, by a foaming waterfall.

Everyone was exhausted. Dave Rand had driven his party along at a ruthless pace, knowing that every yard covered was bringing him closer to his missing children. They'd taken few brief rest stops, and conversation had been kept to a minimum.

Melmoth was lying on his belly, gnawing one of the sticks of jerky. He occasionally snarled at the dried meat as if to make sure it was really dead.

"Tomorrow we'll try and hunt something," said Dave. "Let's share this out and finish it all. Just keep the self-heats for an emergency."

They sat cross-legged on the ground, facing one another. The containers of milk were put in the middle, along with large chunks of bread and the remainder of the strips of jerky.

"Now we can stuff ourselves and make ourselves really sick." Lee grinned.

"And you can tell me about those tents and how you got the food," Edwin prompted.

Zera was dipping her bread into the milk, frowning with concentration. "Sickest people you ever saw, Dr. Kael," she said.

"Hunger?" he asked.

"No. Most of them were bald, kids as well. Teeth falling out, sores all—"

"Around their faces? Especially their mouths? Weak and pale. Probably endemic dysentery." His voice was harsh and the other three stared at him.

"Edwin, what's—"

"That place on the hill you mentioned, Dave. Know what it was, my friends? It was a fast breeder reactor. Everyone in that tented town is dying of radiation sickness. It's in the rocks, the air, the water, the milk, the bread . . . everything's poisoned!''

That night they slept hungry once again.

14

They broke their fast on the self-heats.

"Funny," Lee said. "Last night, after Edwin told us about the radiation sickness, I didn't feel like eating. Yet a minute before that I'd have eaten Melmoth's eyeballs, if they'd been nicely cooked. Now I feel hungry again."

There were six self-heating cans, all dented and without labels.

"Curried beans," said Dave, as the lid peeled back on the first tin.

Lee pressed in the small red button on the top of the fifth can, watching as the second one began to crack itself open. He picked it up carefully and sniffed. "Curried beans."

The third can malfunctioned and overheated, but the charred contents were very familiar. And the fourth and fifth self-heats both contained curried beans.

"Just don't hang around downwind of me," said Edwin Kael. "Still, it's some real good fiber for us all."

THEY FOUND another corpse an hour along the trail, lying sprawled a few paces down the hillside. It was the buzzing horde of glittering blowflies that attracted their attention.

"Can't have been dead more than five or six hours," said Dr. Kael after a cursory examination of the body. "Even at these low temperatures I'd guess very early morning." He started back up to rejoin the others. "Single knife thrust straight through the heart, with a narrow blade. Whoever did the butchering was either very lucky or very skillful."

The man looked to be in his early twenties, short and muscular. Both arms were covered in tattoos whose subject matter was either lewd or military. The corpse had been stripped of everything except the camouflage jacket it wore, which was stiff with dried and drying blood.

Apart from the empty eye sockets, sucked clean by early scavengers, the man could have been lying in careless sleep.

"If we follow them for long enough, they might all finish up by killing one another," said Zera.

THE AIR WAS CLEARER NOW, mainly because the wind had changed direction. It was blowing in from their right, partly at their backs as they trudged on following the tracks of the horsemen. Ahead of them, like a gigantic beckoning finger, they could see a towering column of volcanic smoke. It was dark at the base, mixing black and royal purple, lightening through crimson and orange, shifting nearer its peak to a pale yellow that finally became white, dispersing then into the high clouds.

"That's not far off," Lee said.

They'd stopped briefly by a narrow stream, to drink deep and top up the containers—thoroughly washed out—that had held the tainted milk. Melmoth, too, was lapping at the edge of the stream, red tongue flicking at the fresh, bubbling water. The curried beans had put a layer on their stomachs, holding off the griping pains of hunger, but making them thirsty.

Dave looked to the west through the glasses. "Could be twenty miles. Fifteen at least. Thirty at the outside . . . no, not that far."

Zera was examining the hoof marks in the trampled mud on both sides of the narrow river. "They did a lot of slipping and sliding," she said.

"So?"

She looked at Dave. "You seen much fodder for animals in the past few days? Unless they got some from the tent town, the horses are going to start falling dead under them. The marks show they're getting double-tired."

IT WASN'T LONG after noon when they saw the circling buzzards. They pulled up short after reaching a clearing that reeked of blood and death.

"You were right, Zera," Dave admitted, looking around at the sodden shambles.

Sheever must have realized his animals were nearing the end of the line, and he'd arranged a culling. More than a dozen horses, spavined, ribs almost breaking through their dulled coats, and a solitary mule, lay tangled in frozen death.

"How come we didn't hear the shooting?" asked Lee. "Bullet through the head of each of them. We should've heard that."

"We've been along that stream for the past three miles, then we climbed and came down again. The ridge and the trees would have swallowed up most of the noise."

"They've cut meat from a lot of them," observed Edwin Kacl. "Reckon we might do the same."

"Raw horse meat," said Zera. "You know how to show a girl a real great time."

"We'll have a small fire this evening," Dave said, "after we find a safe place to camp. Cooked horse meat, Zera. Reckon it'll taste good."

They all drew their knives and began to move among the still-warm bodies.

It wasn't a task they relished, but survival had its dictates, and when they moved on, at least they could look forward to an evening meal.

In the afternoon they encountered a huge tangle of fallen trees, impassable even on foot.

"Horses went that way," said Lee, pointing to the right. "Then they came back and went left."

"They must have found the side trail blocked to the right. We go left, and we can narrow the distance between us," Dave said.

By evening he reckoned that they'd actually closed the gap on Sheever's party.

"There's a gap in the brush," Zera reported. "You can see down the track for miles. There's camp fires. Must be their fires."

"Let's go recce," Lee suggested.

Dave shook his head. "No, Lee. Go in in the dark, and you run into his guards. Could take at least three or four hours even to find them. Lose the sight line, and it'd be longer."

"Tomorrow?"

"Could be. We've covered 99.9 percent of the hunt. We don't want to fuck it up in the last little bit. Let's just get our own small fire going and roast some of this delicious meat."

"It's colder again," Edwin said. "Felt a few flakes of snow on the teeth of the easterly."

"That's all we need."

WITHIN AN HOUR the forest lay huddled under several inches of fresh-fallen snow.

Their fire was under overhanging branches, and it lasted long enough to give everybody, including a voraciously grateful Melmoth, a full belly of charred horsemeat.

"Got to find some cover," said Dave.

"Build up the fire," Edwin Kacl suggested.

"Not here," argued Zera.

"Why not? It's a good place. Sheltered."

"Read Jack London, Doc. Story about a dude freezing to death in the Yukon, who lights a fire to save his life. Under trees."

"And?"

The young woman brushed blown flakes of snow from her face. "And it's a blizzard. Snow builds up on the branches of his sheltering tree. Fire melts some of it and it falls down. Goodbye to the fucking fire and goodbye to the guy."

Edwin nodded slowly. "Then we should try and find some shelter."

"We passed a trail a quarter mile back," said Lee. "Melmoth was curious, but we were hurrying on. Looked like someone had gone to the trouble of dragging dead wood and branches over it. Could be a resort home."

"Give this snow another hour, and we won't be able to backtrack with enough accuracy to be safe," said Dave.

"It's only about ten minutes away," said Lee.

In the grinding wind and whiteout conditions, it took them three times that long to reach the area.

They stood silently for a while, waiting for a decision. There was so much snow falling that it wasn't possible to guess how long the side trail had been blocked.

"Could be something up there," Edwin Kael commented, looking at Dave. "Worth a look."

"Better than freezing here." Dave led them around the jumble of branches, noticing when he was on the other side that someone had actually built the break, skillfully binding the dead wood together using thin plastic cords. On the far side there was a loop of the cord that could be used as a handle to heave the whole mass aside.

"Best keep the weapons out and ready," he said to the others.

"Think it could be a trap," said Lee, having to shout to be heard above the rising wind.

Dave didn't know if his son was voicing a suspicion or a question. But he shook his head. "Can't be a trap. There's no way they'd know anyone was coming. More likely we'll take someone by surprise.''

AS DAVE LED the trio of friends up a narrow and winding path, his daughters were less than five miles away from him.

They huddled together in the darkness, trying to avoid catching the eye of Sheever. The giant was in a fearsome rage after having to slaughter half of the livestock during the day when it had become obvious they were traveling more slowly with them than they would without them.

"Think Daddy'll come and find us?" asked Roxanne Rand. It was her favorite question and one that she asked every night and at intervals during the day.

Ellie gave her little sister the same reply every time. "'Course he will, Roxie. One day he'll come and find us."

THE WIND WAS RISING close to hurricane force, and it drove the snow into their faces. Zera had tripped and fallen over a broken branch, turning her ankle. She yelped out with the pain.

"Want me to carry you?" Dave asked.

She stood and leaned on him, grimacing as she took her weight on the right foot. Ice hung from her eyebrows and frosted her mouth. Goggles protected her eyes but the snow was caked on them, making it difficult to see.

"No. I'm okay, Dave. I'll just go slow for a few minutes to walk it off."

Only fifty yards farther on, Melmoth stopped. He gave a cautionary bark, and turning to make sure they'd heard him. Lee grabbed him and snapped on the leash, fumbling with frozen fingers to do up the chrome catch.

The others joined him, peering around. The pit bull had obviously seen or heard something.

"Just keep going," Dave called out, drawing the Linebaugh in his gloved hand, thumbing back on the hammer and readying himself for anything.

"Light," shouted Edwin, pointing ahead of them and a little to the right.

The wind had eased for a few lung-filling seconds, and they could all see the light flickering away in the snowy darkness.

For a moment Dave had a faint memory of a poem, maybe by Robert Frost. Was it about losing yourself in woods, or was it about some task that still needed to be done? It was one of Ellie's favorite poems, and she'd won a recitation prize in third grade for it. And now he couldn't recall the lines anymore.

They closed in on the light. They found the trail widened into a driveway that curved up to a single-story building. The glow came through a chink at the top and side of drawn drapes. Dave could hear the faint pounding of a gas generator from the rear of the trim house.

The four friends were gathered close together. Zera tugged at Dave's sleeve, pulling him toward her so that he could hear. "How do we play it? All go in together?"

"I don't know. There could be a dozen men in there, or there could be one little old lady working away on her crochet with a dry sherry at her elbow."

It was too cold outside to agonize over the fine tuning of a plan. They decided Lee and Zera were to cover the back door of the house. Edwin and Dave would try the front. Any shooting, and they'd all come running.

There was a storm door at the front with a large porch. Dave risked a quick glance around, shielding his lighter in his cupped hand. Apart from a dark maroon parka and a pair of thigh-length black rubber waders, the porch was empty.

He reached out and turned the handle on the main door, finding to his surprise that it opened easily and silently.

"Wait here," he whispered to Edwin. "Sure you don't want the rifle?"

"No. Anyone comes out, I'll talk him to death. Take care, Dave."

Dave was in a heated entrance hall. After the blizzard, the warmth was almost overpowering. The hall was illuminated by a spear of light thrown from an open door to the right. Music was filtering out of the room. Dave recognized the strains of Verdi's *Requiem*.

Dave moved silently along. He glanced behind him once but saw nothing but his trail of wet boot prints on the polished wooden tiles.

He stood near the open door and cautiously leaned sideways to see into the room. The furnishings were comfortable and luxurious. A long sofa faced a fire of logs. He could just see a pair of naked feet and the edge of an embroidered caftan, and the soft crackling from the fireplace spoke of home.

Preceded by the damp muzzle of the handgun, Dave stepped into the room. An attractive woman with very long black hair was lying on the sofa, holding a goblet of what looked like white wine.

She smiled at him. "Hi. Come on in and make yourself comfortable."

"Why not?" he said.

15

Sheever's voice was like the man himself—harsh, bleak and utterly uncompromising. Janine Rand had once said to her daughters that his voice reminded her of two ice-bound granite boulders grinding remorselessly together.

Now he had his two senior lieutenants sitting by his side around the largest of the camp fires. The snow was falling unremittingly. It was not far from midnight.

His hair, so light it was almost white, was tied back in a ponytail, held in place with a black velvet ribbon. His eyes, violet-colored, moved from man to man, seeming to bore clear through them.

"I don't want to hear from you why this is not a good idea. I want you to tell me that tomorrow, once this eternal snow has stopped falling, you will send off four men to do what I want."

The older of the lieutenants, who'd been a sergeant in a special undercover unit, picked at his teeth with a splinter of pine wood. He extracted a hunk of horse meat and flicked it into the fire.

"What if there isn't anyone coming after us?"

Sheever nodded. "Fair question, Lemuel. Could be I'm wrong. But there was that group near the big fire, down at the lake side. Coincidence? Hunters? Innocent people near us?" He reached out and held the man by the wrist, his fingers tightening until Lemuel's face whitened. "There is no such thing as innocent people near us, is there? Is there?"

"No, guess not. We could have gone back after them that night."

"We could have, but we didn't. Where are they now? Are they trailing us for some reason that we cannot comprehend? Better we waste a few hours and move on with merry hearts and a light song upon our lips. Wouldn't you say?"

The fingers relaxed their grip, and Lemuel managed a nod of agreement.

The other man, who was a skinny weapons expert from an airborne group, was quick to get his agreement in before Sheever asked him. "Sure. We'll do it. Soon as the snow stops falling. Tomorrow."

The blond man sighed and looked up, watching the fountain of whirling sparks, carried into the black sky and extinguished by the large flakes of white that still tumbled around them.

"That's good," he said.

KATE MAZURSKY UNCOILED herself from the sofa, brushing a hand through her raven's-wing hair. "Anyone want some more Gewürztraminer? There's two more bottles in the cooler."

"Best we catch up on some rest," said Dave. "Thanks anyway."

Melmoth was lying in front of the smoldering fire, fast asleep. His legs twitched as he chased temptingly succulent prey through rolling summer meadows.

Lee had also dropped off, sprawled in one of the burgundy armchairs. His chin and T-shirt were spotted with sauce from the spaghetti that Kate had cooked for them. Zera and Edwin found their heads nodding forward, too, then they would jerk themselves awake again and blink around the luxurious room with sleepy disbelief.

Dave Rand shared that disbelief.

Kate Mazursky's home was functioning just as though the planet hadn't been devastated by the effects of the asteroid, Adastreia. The gas generator worked smoothly, providing power for lighting and heat. And in the trees immediately behind the house there was a tank of gas that had once held fifteen thousand gallons.

"Last time I checked it there was still about four thou left," she drawled.

"What happens when that runs out?" Dave had asked her.

She'd smiled a lazy, hazed smile, and went into her bedroom. A few moments later she reappeared, holding a small brown bottle in her hand. "Six of those," she'd said. "Best insurance policy a woman could possibly have."

The house belonged to her widowed mother, who had been on an extended vacation in Big Pine Key, south of Florida when the Big Hit came. Kate, who was in her mid-twenties, had heard nothing from her and assumed that the keys had been overwhelmed by tidal waves.

"Mom was a writer. She wrote about the wilderness. That's why she had this place built, to be as far away from people as she could get. But she hated discomfort. This place cost half the defense budget to put together."

Before they went to bed, she gave them a quick tour of the place. It wasn't particularly large, with only two bedrooms, but everything was straight out of the top drawer.

Sauna and Jacuzzi, both indoor and outdoor. A games room with a pool table and a well-stocked bar. Somewhere out back there was a big swimming pool, but without maintenance it had effectively gone back to nature. The furniture was all quality, with a lot of early Colonial pieces. There was a silver salver that was attributed to Paul Revere himself, some superb crystal and lamps by Tiffany and Lalique, the most sophisticated sound and las-vid system that Dave had ever seen, with a library of tapes. A pantry behind the kitchen was half-filled with the best of convenience foods.

"You live really well, Kate," Dave remarked as she walked along the hall with him toward the guest room.

"I don't know that *living* is quite the right word for what I do here."

"Better in here than out there."

"I believe you. But being the hermit of misty mountain is not always the best fun."

As she spoke, she stumbled a little and laid a hand on his arm to steady herself. She smiled, and he could smell the fine wine on her breath.

"Didn't tell you that the hermit was a paid-up drunk, did I, Dave?" she said, laughing to herself. The smile didn't come close to her eyes.

Dave looked at her. Living alone, sealed away in what was almost a consumer's dreamworld, it wasn't surprising that Kate had taken to the bottle with open arms.

"We'll get up early in the morning," he said. "Unless the blizzard still has us locked in."

"You sure that you and the boy'll be all right? And Zera in the living room with the doctor?"

There was an implied question there about his relationship to Zera. And, he realized, something that might have been an invitation to him.

"We're fine as we are. Thanks for everything, Kate."

She put her face up to him, and he kissed her softly on the cheek.

"Sleep well," she breathed.

IT SNOWED ALL NIGHT.

All through the next morning, the flakes kept driving against the double windows of the house. Finally, toward the middle of the afternoon, it began to ease.

Dave stared across the bank of white stretching out behind the building, toward the sunken rectangle where the swimming pool slept. The sky was still the color of riven slate, with a canopy of unbroken cloud from east to west.

Edwin Kael was at his elbow. "Go now?"

"No. We'll spend another night here and get our batteries well charged up. There are rucksacks for us all, and we can carry food with us to last five or six days if we're careful. So we go first thing in the morning and then push on as fast as we can."

"You don't think Sheever might turn around and come after us?"

"Why should he?"

"Lee saw this side trail. Maybe someone else did, too."

"I suppose.... All right, Edwin, we'll keep a watch out tonight. Better safe than sorry."

"One at a time or two at a time?"

"One. I'll work out a schedule."

THE SCOUTING PARTY left Sheever's camp as dusk was falling. Four men, well armed and wearing camouflage jackets. Not that they were much use against the arctic landscape. But at night most cats were black.

IT HAD BEEN a bizarre day.

Lee and Zera had spent much of it crashed in front of the vid and television, playing personal favorites from the tape library. Several times Dave came through and found them fast-forwarding, packing as much sensory experience as they could into the twenty-four stolen hours.

Edwin was content to read, dipping here and there into the collection of leather-bound classics, though he'd been disappointed to find that many of them contained abridged works in a series called "Twenty Great Books in One Volume." The introductions boasted that "A team of the finest literary authorities has edited these great books for your reading pleasure. No longer will it take you a year to plow through *War and Peace*. A fifteen-page plot summary will tell you all you want to know. And more!"

So Dave mostly just sat around, then took a long, lingering hot bath, luxuriating in the costly foaming oil that Kate Mazursky insisted on pouring in for him.

"Passion fruit, jojoba and blueberry," she told him.

All four of them took the opportunity to catch up on their personal laundry, using a range of washing and drying machines. Zera washed her hair, then spent a half hour agonizing whether to allow Kate to cut it for her. She decided in the end that it didn't look too bad as it was.

The storm was over, and darkness was settling around their hideaway when Dave called his team together for a council.

"We're keeping watch tonight. Zera goes first, followed by Lee. Edwin relieves him, and I'll do the last two hours from four until first light."

Kate, sitting on the sofa, clutching a frosted glass of amber liquid, started to giggle. "You 'fraid the big bad wolf'll come and get us?"

"Big bad wolf's already killed my wife and stolen my two daughters," Dave replied, turning on his heels and leaving the room.

THE POINT MAN was on hands and knees, sniffing at the air like a hunting dog. He raised his right hand and beckoned to the others, then used his thumb to indicate that he thought there might be something up the side trail, behind the break of tangled dead wood.

ZERA HAD TURNED sentry duties over to Lee on time.

For the first hour or so, he walked quietly around the sleeping house with Melmoth padding at his heels. Then the pit bull got tired and went back into the living room to take up his adopted position in front of the embers of the fire.

Lee was in the hall, the SIG-Sauer 232 9 mm pistol tucked handy into his belt. He heard a rustle of movement at the end of the hall, near the kitchen.

"Who's that?" he whispered.

"Me. Kate. Just getting myself a nightcap to help me sleep. Want one?"

He suddenly realized that he felt very thirsty. "Yeah. Please."

She vanished again, and he heard the tinkling of ice cubes and glass, the gurgling of liquid. Kate reappeared with a goblet filled with creamy fluid, holding it out for him. She was wearing only a short nightgown of saffron silk, fringed with orange lace. It was low at the neck, loose around the waist. Her black hair was uncoiled across her shoulders.

Lee took the drink and sipped it. There was a taste of chocolate and vanilla, very smooth, overlaid with a hint of something fiery that almost made him cough.

"Thanks . . . real nice, Kate."

She was so close that he could breathe in the feminine taste and scent of her body.

"Drink it all down," she said. "It's nicer that way. There's plenty more. I always have a jug ready-mixed in the fridge."

He drained it, aware that the warm element was quite strong, but it felt soothing to his stomach and gave him a gentle buzz. The sensation was so pleasant that he held out the empty glass for a refill.

"Please."

"Sure."

He sat down on a bench seat in the hall, realizing that the warmth was spreading throughout his body. As the young woman came back from the kitchen, Lee was already standing up, waiting for her.

"Thanks, Kate." He took a healthy slug of the cocktail.

"I call it a Washington Bedwarmer," she said. "Nice name?"

Her hand was on his arm, the fingers sliding along to the elbow, back to his hand, turning it over and rubbing the center of his palm. Her thumb and fingers circled his index finger and rubbed, *very* softly, up and down.

Up and down, then up again.

Up.

"Shit!"

She moved a half inch away from him. "What's wrong, Lee?"

"It's time. I'll be coming for...I mean, Edwin'll be coming to take me...take..."

"Take you in hand, do you mean?" Putting the glass down, she used *her* free hand to explore the tightening front of his jeans.

Lee swallowed hard, backing off. "Not yet. I've got about fifteen minutes or so left on the watch."

"That's all right, love," she said, smiling and licking her lips.

"All right?"

"I'll get you one more Bedwarmer to keep you well...well prepared. I'll go to my room and sort of fool around some."

"Right. Triple-great." Lee had a sudden desire to lay his head on one side and show her how much his face resembled the rising sun. But some part of his befuddled senses told him this wasn't the best idea he'd ever had.

Kate left him with a slow kiss, her tongue probing between his lips, her hand still touching him in a way that challenged his last shreds of self-control. Lee held the third glass of the creamy cocktail and decided he might as well down it in one go. There was no point in waiting, and Edwin was bound to be along soon.

The outer kitchen door opened easily on oiled hinges, allowing a breath of freezing air to insinuate itself into the house. The sensitive thermostat picked up on the temperature change and kicked in the boiler. The hot water in the pipes bubbled and began to circulate again.

Melmoth stirred in his sleep, eyelids twitching, then slipped back into a deeper slumber.

Dave Rand also moved slightly, the fingers of his right hand clenching so his knuckles whitened. But he didn't wake.

Lee was slumped over on the bench seat, the handgun on the floor in the shadows by his feet. The Mamba Blackjack knife was safely sheathed

under his shirt at the small of his back. He was
snoring quietly.

WHEN EDWIN KAEL was wakened by the insistent
buzz of his wrist alarm, it was a couple of minutes
before two o'clock.

As he walked out into the dimly lit hall, his foot
brushed against something heavy and metallic. He
bent and picked up the handgun, conscious of a
draft from the rear of the house.

Not wanting to rouse everyone with a false
alarm, Edwin ran silently into the kitchen, finding
the door wide open. His breath misted around his
mouth as he opened it to shout a warning.

16

Lee was half running, stumbling, falling. He got up again when someone slapped him with casual brutality across the side of his head, making his ears ring. There was blood coming from his nose and mouth, but in his drunken, semiconscious state, he couldn't even remember how it had happened.

He'd been sleeping. Well, resting for a few minutes until . . . until Edwin relieved him and then he and Kate were . . .

"Fucking faster, you gutless piece of shit!" The hissed warning was accompanied by another blow across the face.

Lee was soaking wet from falling and being dragged in the fresh snow covering the patio and back garden of the house. They'd skirted the pool and were close to the fringe of trees and bushes.

He was also freezing.

As he'd been hustled toward the back door, a hand clamped over his mouth, he'd been vaguely aware that one of three—or was it four?—attackers had grabbed his anorak off the peg in the hall. But they hadn't stopped to let him put it on.

He fell yet again and was cursed and kicked to his feet. But now he was facing the back of Kate's elegant, warm home. He managed to focus on the open kitchen door and saw someone come dashing out through it.

And there was a yell of warning, piercingly loud in the stillness of the night.

"Fuck it!"

EDWIN KAEL HAD NEVER fired a gun in his life, had never actually ever held a gun in his hand.

His first, passing surprise was how heavy the automatic was. Loaded with the full charge of seven full metal jacket rounds, it weighed more than two pounds. His second surprise was that it felt oddly comfortable, the ribbed butt setting well into his palm, his first finger easy on the trigger.

As he ran out of the kitchen, he'd seen a group of four men, all wearing brown-and-green-dappled jackets, dragging a fifth figure toward the edge of the snow-crusted bushes, near where the garden ended and the wilderness began.

Edwin couldn't remember what he'd shouted as a warning to Dave and the others. It was just an inarticulate yell of anger and distress.

As soon as he was out in the snow, he realized that the attackers could see him just as easily as he could see them. Slipping and nearly tumbling on the icy ground, he still ran toward them, stopping and opening fire with the SIG-Sauer.

The gun kicked more than he'd expected, but he instinctively copied what he'd seen on vids, and held his right wrist with his left hand to steady it.

He pumped out all seven rounds, continuing to squeeze the trigger again and again after the mag was spent. The hammer rose and fell with a flat, hollow click on the empty chamber.

Though he wasn't aware of it, Edwin's lips peeled back off his white teeth in a feral snarl of hatred and rage.

He heard someone scream and saw a man fall, kicking in the snow. One of the others helped him to his feet while the third one concentrated on hauling Lee into the bushes.

Edwin was only twenty yards away, standing splay-legged, the empty gun loose in his fingers. To his surprise the fourth attacker was running directly for him.

"You come with us, you bastard!" yelled the stocky man, threatening Edwin with a stubby machine pistol. "Fucking now!"

A light came on behind them, flooding the snowy garden with brightness. Someone snapped off a burst of fire, and there was the sound of glass exploding. A voice called something, and the light went off.

Edwin wasn't able to move, feeling oddly outside himself, seeming to see his hand open and the gun drop in the snow. Then he was being hustled along, fingers gripping him hard at the elbow. A voice maintained a constant flow of foul language to encourage him after Lee.

The wounded man was lurching from side to side, moaning, doubled over, clutching at his stomach.

"Fast, before they..."

The leader of the gang was right at Edwin Kael's elbow, turning back to the dark house to cover any potential threat. His face was close to the black doctor, scowling at him, the muzzle of his Uzi menacing him.

Edwin didn't even hear the rifle.

All he knew was that the pale blur at his side had exploded.

Blown apart, as if someone had just detonated some nitro in the center of the man's skull. The face disappeared and warm blood and brains showered over Edwin and the others. There was just enough light for him to see that one of the eyes had gone from its socket, and the nose and most of the left cheek had completely disappeared. Something stung his own face, and he guessed he'd probably been cut by shards of flying bone from the dead man.

The body crumpled in a tangle of arms and legs, nearly knocking Edwin over.

Back at the house, Dave tried to sight in on another of the men. But they were among the bushes now. At the last moment one turned and sprayed the side of the building with a prolonged burst from a machine pistol.

Then there was only an aching stillness.

"WE HAVE TO GO after them," Zera insisted.

"No point. You chase armed men through open country at night and you end up fucking dead," Dave replied.

Kate was sitting with them, one arm drunkenly around the pit bull. The house was in total darkness, and they were in the living room. Dave had pulled the drapes halfway across, covering the broken glass, but cold air still flooded in. He refused to allow Kate to close the shutters or put on any light.

"We'll freeze," she complained.

"Better than being shot."

"But they've gone."

"Maybe."

"They've got the nice black guy and your cute son, and you just—"

Dave turned to look at her, his face barely visible in the gloom. "Why don't you shut your fucking wide mouth?"

THE FEAR that Sheever would return with more of his men haunted Dave. To stay in Kate Mazursky's home was to invite the trap, but to go out into the bleak country was a worse option. He decided that once light came, he'd track down the men who'd raided them. But not before dawn.

As the darkness finally retreated, it showed the corpse of the man who'd been hit, sprawled and frozen, surrounded by a blackened patch of bloodied snow. A trail of splattered drops revealed that at least one of the other men had been wounded. Unless the blood came from either Edwin or Lee...

The assault had been too quick and too confusing for Dave to be sure of anything. He only knew that a part of his heart had been torn away, and his sole driving ambition now was to find Sheever and kill him.

Zera would come with him. That was something that he'd never questioned for a moment.

But he was surprised when Kate Mazursky also insisted on coming along with them.

17

Lee was bitterly embarrassed to find that he'd wet himself.

Fortunately, their escape was such a wild chase through deep snow that every one of them was soaking wet by the time they struggled into the camp.

Dawn wasn't far off, but Lee noticed that the sentries were patrolling with a military precision. They yelled out a warning as soon as they heard the party crashing along the narrow trail toward the well-sited camp.

A minute or so later, Lee and Edwin were face-to-face with Sheever. Though face to face was hardly an accurate description. The blond giant was a scrape more than seven feet tall.

Lee looked anxiously around the group of men who were filtering toward them, most rubbing sleep from their eyes. Nearly all wore vestiges of army gear, and he realized that the secondhand information about the gang being military deserters looked to be correct.

There was no sign of either of his sisters.

Lee had the dreadful fear that if they suddenly say him, one of them—probably Roxanne—would blurt out their relationship. Even before he saw Sheever close up, it seemed a dangerous situation. Now, standing and shivering in front of the giant, Lee thought he might throw up.

The injured man, gut-shot by Edwin Kael, had fallen to the dirt and was moaning loudly. Blood seeped between his clasped hands and his face was parchment-pale.

"This boy needs a coat," said Sheever to nobody in particular. Someone handed Lee his anorak without a word, and he gratefully shrugged it on. "And someone should look to poor Raymond. Seems as if he has a nasty wound in his abdomen."

Sheever had a skin like milk, with only a trace of fine silver stubble along the line of his massive jaw. His eyes, under snowy brows, were a strange light violet color. He wore a pair of cream leather trousers and a white silk shirt, with a black leather fringed jacket slung over his shoulders. There was a holster on either side of a hand-tooled belt, but Lee couldn't see what sort of guns filled them.

"You're one of the group that's been trailing me, aren't you?"

The voice was pitched quiet, but had a strange, grating quality to it. Lee forced himself to look straight back into the hypnotic eyes.

"No." As an afterthought, he added, "Sir."

"Well . . . I'll ask that one again, later, son."

The man on the ground had started to roll around, his moans rising up a sharp scale to screams. Sheever looked around. "Quiet him," he said, and his orders were immediately followed through. A hunk of rag was unceremoniously stuffed into the man's mouth, muffling the cries.

Sheever turned to Edwin Kael. "And you are also one of those following us to—" He stopped and leaned forward. A hand the size of a baseball glove reached out and held Edwin by the throat, forcing his head to one side. "Well, well . . . the nigger who claimed to be a man of medicine. Kyle, wasn't it?"

"Kael, Mr. Sheever. Edwin Kael."

Sheever nodded. "I don't give a single spit in the wind for who you are, nigger. But you're living proof that we've been trailed from Altmann. Maybe longer. I'll have to wait and talk to the boy about that."

"He's not with me," said Edwin. "His name's Rick Mazursky. Brother of the lady who owns the house you raided."

"Truly?"

"Yeah."

The eyes turned again toward Lee, with only the mildest curiosity in them. "This true, Rick? What the nigger says?"

"It's true, sir."

Sheever sighed. "You gun down Raymond here, nigger?"

"Hope so."

"Cure him."

"What?"

"If you are hard of hearing, Dr. Nigger, then I'll cut off your ears to assist you. I said that you were to heal this poor man."

Edwin Kael looked down. "He's got a bullet smack through the guts. Been bleeding for some time with it. Bullet's still in there, since I don't see an exit wound."

Sheever sounded bored. "So?"

"So...take me back in time a couple of years and put me in charge of a team of top-rated paramedics in a first-class hospital. And I'd have a chance— only a slim one—of saving him."

"Try."

"Pointless."

"Try, nigger. He dies, then you die. And this young man, Mr....what was the name again, son?"

The question suddenly snapped out like a striking prairie rattler.

"Mazursky, sir. Rick Mazursky."

The pale eyes searched his face. Lee swallowed hard, hunching his shoulders protectively. The great head swam in front of him like a midnight ghost, and the boy shivered.

"Cold, Rick?"

"Yeah, sir. And hungry."

"Then you're about the same as all the rest of us. Cold and hungry, is that not so, my men?"

There was a grumble of assent from the sullen gang surrounding them. Lee was trying surreptitiously to count them, but they kept moving. Sheever didn't miss anything.

"Twenty-one of us, Rick Mazursky. Not that you will be able to pass that information on to any of your chasing friends, will you? No."

With his great height, Sheever could see way over the heads of his men. He suddenly pointed and called out, making everyone's head turn.

"I thought I saw a guard come in from patrol to see what the fuck was going on. If I did, then that man will have his lungs torn out and draped around his disgusting neck."

Though he couldn't see anything, Lee heard a scuffle of feet and a ripple of laughter. Sheever patted Edwin Kael on the shoulder, making him flinch.

"Time you got to doctoring, nigger."

"He's dying."

"The beats of his heart run parallel to yours, Dr. Kyle."

"Kael."

Lee was looking around the men, and saw a face peeking between two of them, on the far side of the fire, staring inquisitively to find out what was happening.

It was Ellie.

Lee blinked, swung his head away, then reluctantly back again.

The firelight played off his sister's face, making it shift and change. Ellie had altered in ways that Lee couldn't begin to define. She was still the same teenager he'd known and played with and fought with and loved for all his life, but so...so different.

Her face was thinner, and her brown eyes deeper set. A smear of dirt crossed her forehead, and he noticed a healing scar on the line of her jaw. Her hair looked as though it had been cut with a pair of garden shears and dangled over her temples in a ragged fringe.

She looked an eternity older.

Lee shook his head and lowered his eyes, hoping against hope that she'd take the hint.

Sheever caught the movement. "What're you doing, Rick?"

"Feel sick and I got a headache and—" He let himself go limp, sliding to the earth, nose inches from the toes of the giant's army boots.

"Let him lie," said Sheever. "Boy's not going anywhere for a while. Doctor, you'd better see to your patient."

Lee squeezed an eye open a fraction and peeped to where Ellie had been standing. But his sister had vanished again.

Above him the sky was already lightening, showing patches of blue-pink, with the promise of better weather for the day.

"LOTS OF BLOOD," said Kate Mazursky.

"It looks like Edwin hit one of the bastards with Lee's 9 mm. Nasty wound."

The SIG-Sauer, reloaded, was in Kate Mazursky's belt. There had been a small arsenal of weapons in her house, but she'd chosen to carry Lee's automatic. Compared to the rough clothes worn by Dave and Zera, those of the young woman created a poem in elegance: a light green anorak and thermal-lined tracksuit pants tucked into gleaming black waterproof boots.

Dave was constantly aware of the possibility that Sheever's men might be waiting to ambush them. But the scrambled trail and the blood made him feel more secure that the enemies were traveling at their best speed toward their camp.

The air was filled with the pungent reek of volcanic sulfur, and the sky to the west was a threatening yellowish purple. A couple of times, as they pushed up over the crust of melting snow, Dave Rand thought he caught the faint sound of volcanic rumbling from far ahead of them.

"What do we do when we get there?" Zera asked as they paused for a five-minute break.

"Kill everyone we have to and rescue anyone we can," said Dave.

LEE HAD GLIMPSED both his sisters, sitting in front of a small pup tent, holding on to each other. They were locked in a seemingly intense conversation and seemed to be deliberately not looking up. Roxanne appeared tiny and frail.

The weather had deteriorated drastically in the past twenty minutes. The light promise of the dawn had been replaced by low, heavy cloud, flavored with sulfur, coming in from the west. There was also a distant sound like thunder.

A space had been cleared in front of one of the smoldering fires, and Edwin Kael was kneeling there beside the gut-shot man, Raymond, who was lying on a stained sleeping bag, moaning more quietly than before. His clothes had been cut away from his upper body and his trousers had been unzipped and pulled down over his muscular thighs. Unable to look away, Lee watched his friend struggling to save Raymond's life, knowing that it was already a lost battle.

The gang, heavily armed, stood or sat in a rough half circle, watching in near silence. Sheever himself loomed directly behind the black doctor, arms folded across the barrel of a chest.

Lee took the opportunity to edge away a little, realizing that he was being virtually ignored. Off to the left, beyond where his sisters were sitting, he could see the line of horses, tied to a length of rope between two pines. There was also a cache of stacked weapons, including grenade launchers, and a tripod-mounting heavy machine gun.

He turned, on the edge of the ring of watchers, and looked back at Edwin.

Raymond was kicking, blood streaking his thighs, clotting in the tangle of dark pubic hair. The loop of gray intestine had been pushed back through the entry wound in his stomach. Bright scarlet blood was trickling from his mouth, and his eyes were squeezed shut.

Edwin turned his head to look at Sheever. "I'm really trying, but he's slipping away."

The huge blond man didn't move a muscle to acknowledge the words.

Lee glanced around, wondering if there was any way he could get his hands on a gun and maybe stage a dramatic rescue.

Beyond the cluster of men he could see the far side of the valley, rising to a jagged ridge. The hollows of the mountain were filled with snow. Over the peak, he noticed huge clouds of dust smearing the sky, indicating that the distant eruption was gathering momentum.

The wounded man jerked convulsively, arms flailing, head strained back as though he were being tortured on the rack. He coughed, and a great lump of blood-filled pink froth burst from the gaping jaws. As Edwin reached to try and hold him, the man shuddered and then slumped back.

Then he lay still.

There was a whisper of movement, and the circle of watchers seemed to take a couple of steps inward, as though they'd all heard the same secret signal.

Sheever slowly unfolded his arms.

Lee heard a collective sigh from the watchers, as though they were about to participate in a religious ritual they'd witnessed before.

The hands swooped down like great birds of prey and fastened around the skinny neck of Edwin Kael. There wasn't time for him to utter a single squeak of protest. With no visible effort, Sheever lifted him from the ground, holding him out at arms' length.

Edwin's legs, dangling in the faded trousers of his suit, kicked and kicked and kicked. His hands tried to grapple with Sheever, but the giant's power was awesome. Slowly the fingers tightened, and Edwin's mouth screamed silently. His tongue protruded, blackened, and his eyes began to stand out from their sockets.

Lee couldn't believe what he was seeing. Deliberate, callous and brutal murder. He glanced sideways, realizing that nobody was watching him. Everyone's eyes were locked on the demonstration of butchery.

Sheever exerted all his strength in a great savage thrust of power. There was the loud crack of Edwin Kael's spine snapping. His body went into a spasm, and Sheever cast it from him, like someone throwing away an old coat. "I warned you, Dr. Kyle," he said in his soft, grating voice. "There is no success like failure, and failure means a reserved seat on the last train.''

Lee reached around and drew the Mamba Blackjack knife from the back of his belt and sliced through the rope to which the restless horses were tied, whooping and slapping at them to spook them. They wheeled around wildly, surging at a gallop through the camp.

He stopped for a moment to watch the success of his plan. Through the spray and mud and running men, he caught a glimpse of two things.

One was Ellie and Roxanne, standing together, staring toward him. He half lifted a hand to them, but they didn't make a move in response.

The other thing Lee Rand saw was the face of Sheever. The giant hadn't moved, allowing the horses to rush past him on either side, as if he were a stone breakwater that divides the foaming waves. But his violet eyes locked on Lee's, his face showing no emotion.

The boy had the feeling that his image was being stored away inside the monumental head, filed, ready to be drawn out again when the moment was right.

It took a great effort for Lee to start running into the darkness of the surrounding forest.

Toward his father.

18

"But how did they look?"

"I told you."

"Again, Lee. Tell me again."

"I saw them for a few seconds, quite a long way off. They're both alive. Dirty and hungry-looking. That's all I can say."

"What were they wearing?"

Lee took a couple of steps away from his father, shaking his head. "Look, I know they're your daughters. They're my sisters as well. But Edwin's *fucking dead!*"

Dave took a step toward his son, knuckles clenched. He felt an unfamiliar red mist of anger swoop down on his mind and wanted nothing more at that moment than to slap the boy across the face and rattle his teeth.

Lee saw the rage and half raised a hand against the blow he thought was coming.

But Dave shook his head and even managed something that came close to a smile. "No. Shit, no. I'm sorry, Lee...really."

"It's all right, Dad. I understand. But that's all there is to tell you. I saw them, and they didn't look too bad. I saw Sheever, and he's the most cold and evil fucker I ever saw."

Zera sat on a tree stump, picking away at a leprous fungus that partly covered it. "I just can't believe we won't ever see Edwin again," she said.

But that wasn't quite true.

They saw him one more time, later that same day.

THE BODY LAY more or less where Lee had last seen it. It had fallen at the edge of one of the dying camp fires, and the feet and lower legs had been burned away, showing blackened flesh and charred bones. But the rest was untouched, and at a quick glance it almost looked as if Edwin Kael was quietly sleeping.

Only the crooked angle of the head on the shoulders whispered its testimony to Sheever's brute strength and brutish nature.

There was no sign of the body of Raymond, the man Edwin had shot.

Kate and Zera wanted to bury the corpse. Lee agreed with them, pointing out that the doctor's death had been a direct result of his willingness to accompany them on their rescue mission.

"That's right," said Dave. "And if he could speak, he'd want us to keep going as fast as we can.

Try and bury someone in this permafrost, and it'd take us two...three hours. And then the scavengers would still dig it up."

"We can't leave him like this," Zera insisted. "It's inhuman."

"Times are inhuman, Zera. If they weren't, then we wouldn't be chasing this bastard killer halfway across the bastard continent. You want to say a quick prayer, then do it."

It was Kate who knelt in the trampled mud of the deserted camp, eyes closed, hands together, leading the others. "Lord, accept into Thy arms Thy servant, Edwin Kael, slain by the wicked when seeking only to aid the afflicted. Give him eternal peace. Amen."

"Amen," said the others, with Dave a beat behind Lee and Zera.

"Now let's get going," Dave said. "And everyone take extra care."

THE EVIDENCE of serious volcanic activity grew more and more obvious. The sky was a yellowish pall from east to west, and lightning kept flashing off the peaks all around. The air tasted so foul that the travelers tied cloths around their mouths to make breathing easier.

"We must be very close to them," Dave said, stooping to check some fresh horse droppings.

"It probably took them some time to round up the horses," Lee suggested. "Heavy wooded trail like this, they might be around the next corner."

Melmoth had been ranging a long way ahead of them, occasionally scurrying back to make sure they hadn't tricked him and turned off. But in the past hour he'd been keeping closer, and Dave had the feeling that this might be a sign that the white-haired giant was close.

"Now you've escaped, Sheever's bound to believe there's people after him," Dave said to Lee. "He lost two men and you got away. He's not going to like that, is he? So at some point soon he's going to have a bite at us. Got to. Only question is when."

The wind had veered a little, carrying the worst of the sulfur fumes in a more southerly direction. But every step in pursuit of Sheever took them nearer to the heart of the rumbling volcanic action.

By dusk they'd moved into a region of narrow, steep-sided valleys, like a series of gigantic knife slashes across the land. Most of them had flowing water in them, varying from foaming streams five feet across to tumbling rivers a hundred feet wide.

They were trailing along the side of one of the wider rivers when the attack came.

Melmoth reacted fastest, snarling, nose up, head pointing across the valley. The others heard the sound he'd heard only a fraction of a second later. A high-pitched whistling, growing louder and nearer, the pitch altering as it closed on them.

"Get down!" yelled Dave, throwing himself flat among the rounded boulders at the edge of the clear water.

The mortar shell landed nearly a hundred yards upstream from them. It burst with a great whomp of sound, throwing up a fountain of spray. Fragments of shrapnel whined overhead, skittering off the wet rocks.

"Under cover!"

Dave led the way. The firing of the first of the mortars reached him as he began to move. It overlapped with a second shell that landed less than thirty yards away, which meant Sheever and his men had at least two powerful, long-range weapons. Lee hadn't been able to find out how many there'd been.

Apart from a pair of 40 mm grenade launchers, Sheever also had two heavy .50-caliber machine guns in his armory. And they both opened fire simultaneously, the bullets ripping into the bushes at the edge of the water.

It was nearly a perfect ambush, but the big man had misjudged the moment. Only by about thirty seconds, but that was enough. In another half minute the four figures below him would have been engaged in fording the river and would have been sitting ducks.

Now, they were able to get back into the trees, safe from anything except a lucky shot.

Lee had the Sauer 120 Lux, and he flattened himself behind a huge sycamore and started shooting back. A pall of drifting smoke, close to the top of the hillside opposite, showed where their attackers were firing from.

"Hold it, son, hold it," Dave called. "They might spot the muzzle-flash and pinpoint us. And there's too big a difference in range between what they've got up there and what we've got down here."

Two more mortar shells came thumping down, one behind them in the trees and the other close to the edge of the river. And one of the HMGs opened up, raking along the bushes that bordered the water. The air seemed filled with screaming lead and flying splinters.

Dave buried his head in his hands, cowering against the bedlam, trying to push himself into the soft earth beneath him. It was the first time in his life that he'd had anything like this experience, and it scared the shit out of him.

More than anything it was like an old war-vid about Thailand or Korea or Vietnam.

There was a brief lull.

"You said they looked like real military, Lee?" he shouted, wincing at the way his voice cracked up the scale.

"What?"

"You said they all looked military?"

"Yeah."

"Suppose this shooting was just to cover up an attack from a different direction. That would be the sort of thing they might come up with."

"Don't—" Another mortar shell, this time well short. It released a great cloud of dense, acrid smoke that began to billow toward them.

"Hadn't we better get out?" Zera was coughing as she called to Dave.

"Fuck," Dave swore softly at himself. He felt bitterly angry as he realized for the first time what a weak position they were in. Despite having good handguns and a rifle and scattergun, he knew the enemy were light-years ahead of them. It was comparable to going with a stick against a man armed with an Uzi.

The next sweeping fire from the two machine guns came much closer, and fragments of shattered stone hit the trunk of the tree only inches from Dave's face.

Zera shouted again as soon as the shooting stopped. "Can't we get the fuck out of here?"

"Yeah, yeah. Pull out."

There was a moment of concern after they'd sprinted a couple of hundred yards back up the trail.

"Where's Melmoth?" Kate Mazursky said, panting.

"Thought he was with you, Lee," said Dave. "I haven't seen him since the shooting started."

"Me either. Hey, Melmoth! Melmoth, here boy!" Lee looked around into the blank walls of the pines and birches.

"There he is." Zera pointed.

Bedraggled, tail between his legs, the pit bull came skulking out of the undergrowth. When Lee made a fuss of him and patted him, the dog perked up a little, but kept looking around them, back at the river, where the noise of the assault was beginning to fade away.

"What now?" Kate asked.

Dave wiped sweat from his forehead, tasting salt on his tongue. The closer they got to the volcanic area, the warmer the weather became.

"No brilliant plan, Kate. Only thing is…the trail forked a mile back, and it looked like a way down south, toward the river. Might link up one valley farther along from where Sheever and his gang are. If we can come in parallel, we could even find ourselves ahead of them."

Lee stood, rubbing his hands against his pants to dry them. "We could also lose them completely, Dad."

Dave took a slow, deep breath. "That's right. We could lose them completely."

19

There was a decent moon that night, and Dave decided they should make use of it and extend their traveling time.

"I'm still worried that Sheever will try to ambush us. He might have his men backtrack and hit us during the night again. If that happens, it could mean we're done for."

"If we can get across the river, we should be safe from that." Lee grinned. "Could be us doing the ambushing, huh, Dad?"

"Not with the guns we've got."

"We could get close."

"Twenty trained and well-armed men won't be taken just like that. Not now when they know we're trailing them."

Lee nodded. "Suppose so. But if we did have some long-range weapons, there'd be a risk to Ellie and Roxanne."

Dave had considered that, but had pushed the thought away to the rear of his mind. All along, ever since reading Janine's damp-stained postcard back in California, aeons ago, he'd never really had anything that approximated to an orderly plan. Just the blind drive to go after the girls.

Thousands of miles and many months later, that still just about summed up his campaign.

SHEEVER CALLED Ellie and Roxanne into his tent that night and made the girls stand side by side before his small gas heater. He lounged on his quilted sleeping bag, wearing only shorts and a dark blue sweatshirt.

"Good evening, my dears. You're probably wondering why I've called you here like this." There was no answer, and he sat up and pointed at Ellie. "Aren't you?"

"Yes, Sheever."

"Boldly spoken, child. I don't want to have to be nasty to you, but I have a question, about the business this morning with the nigger and the skinny lout who drove off our horses." He stopped and stared into the white, hissing core of his heater. The sisters had seen him drift away like this before, and they knew better than to risk interrupting him. He finally spoke again. "Now, the nigger came from Altmann. But this boy, what of him? Did either of you see him? I think you must have."

Ellie answered. "We both did, Sheever."

"And?"

She looked puzzled. "Sorry..."

He smiled, showing his teeth. "You *will be* sorry, Ellie Rand. Unless you step as lightly as if your dainty feet rested on the shells of the eggs of a skylark. Did you recognize the boy?"

"No."

He turned his pale, hooded eyes to the younger girl. "And you, Roxie? Did you know him? Or had you heard the name of Rick Mazursky before?"

"Never, Sheever." It was loudly and clearly spoken.

The giant sighed. "Truth or lie? I could always tell when your mother was lying to me. Always. But you two..."

"It's the truth, Sheever," said Ellie.

"Perhaps it is. Paranoia is always the lot of the great leader. But I think I'll send a few men back first thing in the morning to see what they can see."

"Can we go, Sheever, please?" asked Roxanne, gripping her sister by the hand.

"Yes, you can." They turned together to leave the tent with its feral animal smell of the man's sweating body. "No, not you, Ellie. You stay here. Roxanne, go and wait in your own little tent. Your sister will rejoin you in a while."

DAVE'S GUESS had been correct.

The side trail took them down a steep, sliding path to the river. There was enough light from the sailing moon for them to cross a narrow gap between massive gnarled boulders, their hearts in their mouths at the leap over the singing deeps of the water.

The route Sheever had taken was away to their right, but they followed a faint, winding track up the facing slope of the mountain, a mile or so to the south.

There was a flurry of snow in the early hours of the morning, but it didn't accumulate and the ground grew steadily muddier and more slippery.

"It's getting warmer, Dad," Lee said, as they stopped for one of the five-minute breaks they took every hour.

"Must be something to do with that volcano ahead of us."

The actual mountain that was erupting was still hidden from them by the nearer peaks, but the smoke and stench were growing ever thicker, and they could see an occasional fountain of fire and sparks hurled into the night sky.

As they moved higher they began to find more evidence of the earth's anger. A great swath of trees had been blasted to destruction, looking almost as if they'd been scalded to death.

"Think this is safe?" Kate asked, the first time she'd spoken for a couple of hours. The trail had taken its toll on her fashionable hiking gear. Jacket and pants were crumpled and dirty, her gleaming boots filthy and smeared with mud. But she pushed on without any complaint.

"Safe?" Dave replied. "Safe would be sitting in your warm room with a glass of ninety proof in your hand. This is dangerous."

She grinned broadly. "Safe was getting boring."

ZERA SPOTTED the highway around four in the morning. She pointed to where it zigged and zagged along the side of the mountain to their left, down toward the far valley.

Dave followed it with the glasses, seeing that it had been cut close to the top by a great earth shift. The bottom of the valley was still in shadow, and he couldn't make out much. But it looked like another blockage and...

"Something down there," he said, trying to find a sharper focus.

"What? Buildings?" asked Zera.

"Something glass, reflecting the moon. A house or maybe a vehicle."

"Worth going down for a look?"

Dave glanced at his son. "Could be. Let's get closer and check it out."

"ARMY TRUCKS."

The shadows still made it difficult to see precisely what had happened beside the river at the valley bottom. But Dave could see five trucks, in poor condition but showing enough insignia to give them military provenance.

Melmoth was becoming excited, and Dave stooped to calm him down.

"Any people?" asked Zera.

"No sign."

"We going down?"

"It won't take us long, and it looks like we can pick up this trail a little farther along."

"I'VE NEVER SEEN anything like..." Lee's normally loud voice was hushed by an almost religious awe at what they'd found.

"I have," Kate stated casually, rubbing her finger over the smooth surface of a truck door.

"Where?"

"My mother liked vids of disasters. Had one of some big volcano in about 1980 or something. Mount Saint Helens, I think. It blew out and sent jets of superheated steam for miles. Blasted everything and stripped it clean, killed every living creature for miles around like this."

Her suggestion made sense. The trucks had lost most of their paint, and the canvas off the backs had been shredded into oblivion. It was obvious from down in the valley that the shifts in the earth had trapped the small convoy, and then there had been some sort of eruption that had destroyed them.

And killed all the troops in a single searing breath.

There were seventeen dead soldiers, all reduced to skeletons, untouched by scavengers. Those had presumably also perished in the holocaust of fiery steam. The dead lay where they had died, with limbs twisted and contorted, giving a dreadful clue to the terrible pain of their passing.

Apart from the macabre curiosity of the multiple deaths, Dave was interested in what the vehicles might have been carrying.

The answer came shortly. "Nothing," said Lee, hopping down from the tailgate of the last truck. "Looks like they were on their way to pick up something, or heading back to base after making a delivery."

"How about inside the cabs?" Dave suggested.

Zera jumped up in the front of the lead truck, pushing a skeleton out of the way and foraging in the musty interior. Suddenly she whooped out, "Keying fuck-critical, friends!"

The next second she was waving around a snub-nosed, silenced submachine gun, with an integral laser sight.

"Heckler & Koch MP 8," said Dave, recognizing the conventional military weapon. "Triple burst, semi or full auto, 9 mm."

Lee took the gun from Zera and looked at it. "Not much use to us, Dad."

"You mean long-range use?"

"Be good at thirty to fifty yards. They outrange us by a half mile."

"But we're not coming across open ground. If we push on, we can coldcock them. And this is as good as we can look for. How many?"

"Four. Plenty of spare mags on the dash. Not harmed by the steam."

Dave cradled the gun. "Four of these. Hit them when they're together, all on full auto. Massacre the bastards and not risk Ellie or Roxanne either."

SHEEVER SENT OUT his six most efficient killers, mounted on the best horses they had left. He and the rest of the group pushed on westward, seeking the canyon where they could hole up for the winter, near food supplies.

The half dozen came back two days later, riding along a tortuous and steep trail, to report total failure to their leader.

"Tracked them to a fork that went down to the river," said a skinny Mexican man who'd been in charge of the termination group. "I think they crossed, but it started to snow again, and there was no way we could find them. They might have crossed back and still be following us, hidden while we went by. Can't be sure."

Sheever didn't say anything in reply. He simply nodded and went to sit alone by one of the fires.

But his eyes turned again and again to the two young sisters, as though they held the answer to a question that bothered him.

DAVE'S GUESS AND HOPE had been that the trail they were following would eventually connect with the one Sheever and his party had taken.

The biggest problem was the wind, which had once more shifted, blowing the stinking detritus in their direction from the volcano that was now only two or three miles away. The noise from the eruption was nearly deafening, making normal conversation impossible.

Slogging on over the endlessly difficult terrain made them sweat, the perspiration coursing through caked masks of yellow dust.

Melmoth was so reluctant to continue that Lee had been forced to put him on the leash and drag him along.

On the second night Zera came to Dave, where he was sleeping on the ground a few yards from Lee and Kate. They made hasty, unsatisfactory love together, interrupted near their culmination by a particularly savage rumbling from the volcano. Flames streaked hundreds of feet in the air, turning night to day. As they lay clasping each other, there was a faint pattering sound among the upper branches of the trees around them.

"What was that?" she whispered, feeling an almost uncontrollable urge to giggle.

"Must be small stones from the eruption. Much closer, and it could start to get real hot."

She kissed him on the lips, tasting sulfur on his skin. "Tell you one thing about making love here, Dave."

"What?"

"You get a guarantee that you'll feel the earth move."

AS THE PATH CLIMBED higher the next morning, Dave took charge of the miserable pit bull, allowing Lee to go ahead on point, with a warning to scout with extra care. They looked to be nearing the point where their trail might intersect with the one from the north.

Lee was a hundred yards ahead of the others, dropping to hands and knees as he neared the crest of the ridge.

While they watched him, he peered over the top, then slithered hastily back, waving his hands in a furious warning.

20

"We've done it!" he shouted, cupping his hands to his mouth so that they could hear him above the pounding rumble of the volcano.

"Done what? Are they there?"

Lee's lean face was alight with excitement. "I can see them. Saw Sheever on his horse. They're about a mile or more down and to the right. We can get over the ridge and in front of them without being seen!"

Now that the end was so close, Dave felt curiously flat.

He coughed at the fumes that seemed inescapable. "If that volcano blows big, there's going to be baked and steamed meat from here to Seattle."

"At least we'll all die together," Zera said.

Kate shook her head. "No. That's not true. When we go, each of us goes alone. Right at the end, we all go alone."

Dave led them back to the top of the hill, raising his head with infinite care to avoid being skylined from below. But other peaks rose behind them, and there was scant chance of being seen.

His son's guess had been about right. Standing out against the stained land was Sheever's milk-white stallion, picking its delicate way up the trail. The rest of Sheever's group stretched out behind him. Dave could just spot the girls, riding two-up on a chestnut mare, around the middle of the line.

The geography of the immediate region was complicated and potentially dangerous. With the extra height, Dave and his three companions could see a great deal farther than Sheever.

The spur of the mountain where Dave hid ran to the west but didn't connect up immediately with the Sheever trail. Although the blond giant didn't yet know it, since he rode without scouts, that track was completely blocked off a quarter mile ahead, around a blind corner. Half the peak had fallen, slicing the road away as with a butcher's cleaver.

But there was a rough track winding steeply down and then trekking up again, running parallel to the ridge Dave and the others were on. Eventually the two parties would meet, but Dave had a clear advantage on time.

The wild card was the volcano.

Now they could see it clearly, belching out smoke and filth, occasionally giving a shattering roar and producing cascades of fire a thousand feet high. The liquid rock was flowing from the far side of the cone, the southwesterly wind taking it away from the two parties of human beings who were probably the only living things for twenty miles.

"Not much cover," Dave muttered, raking the ground with the glasses for any sign of a good ambush site.

"There's a sort of narrow path up there," Kate said, pointing to the left of where the main tracks finally intersected. It wound directly along the bottom of the volcano.

"Yeah." He squinted, wiping his eyes to clear them of the pervading grit. "Could be the working of an old mine? But Sheever would never go up there. Main route strikes higher and ahead. He'd suspect danger."

"What if he saw me, running away, like I was trying to escape?"

"No." Dave's denial of Kate's suggestion was flat and final. "Much, much too risky. If he didn't take the bait then we could never save you."

The young woman persisted. "But if he *did* buy it? Then I could bring them in close enough for you to massacre them with these new guns, couldn't I? I could, Dave."

"No." But Dave's answer was less flat and not quite so final.

THE ONLY CHANGE to Kate's plan Dave had insisted on was for him to act as decoy, not Kate.

"I'm fitter, stronger, can run faster, and they're my daughters," he said.

"I'm younger, nearly as fit and strong, and if I get killed, I don't leave two girls without a father."

"Couldn't let you do it."

"You wouldn't be *letting* me do it, you pompous male prick! It's my idea, and I want to do it."

"No. And if we hang around here arguing, then Sheever'll be on top of us, and the plan'll be too bastard late."

"I could do it, Dad," Lee volunteered.

"I'll do it, Lee. Now we've got—"

"Let me do it, Dave."

"Zera, just shut up. And you, too, Lee. We'll get close to the fork and then separate. Finalize the plans for the actual ambush when we're there. Lee, you keep an eye on Melmoth."

THE BLOCKAGE OF THE TRAIL brought Sheever to the edge of one of his homicidal, psychotic rages.

"Lemuel!"

"Yo, Sheever?"

"You said we didn't need anyone out point? Now we all have to turn around and ride back down the fucking hill."

Lemuel had seen Sheever vent his anger on other members of their unit. It was never a pleasant sight.

"That way?" he said, pointing with a gauntleted hand into the shadowed bottom of the valley.

At that moment the volcano, now perilously close to them, gave a spectacular coughing outburst, making the horses skitter sideways. Tiny pebbles danced off the trail around them, and Lemuel felt one land on the crown of his hat. He reached up and removed it, holding it in his palm, watching the leather of his glove begin to smolder from the fragment of stone. Before he flicked it to the mud, it had cooled from cherry-red to a dull gray.

The distraction served to shift Sheever's rage away, and the big man craned his neck, watching the enormous pillar of pallid yellow smoke as it soared into the waiting clouds.

"Down and then up again. Why not, Lemuel? Yeah, why not?"

THE LAND WAS utterly lacking any sort of vegetation. Even the tiniest weeds had been blasted to extinction by the heat and poisonous fumes.

Dave guessed that the temperature had to be closing on 77 Fahrenheit, warmer than he'd been since before the Big Hit.

The crest of the hill kept Sheever well out of sight, but it wasn't possible for him to make it to the top in less than another hour. There was time to settle the arrangements for the last scene of the drama.

"Those old buildings'll do us fine," Dave said. "We can wipe away Sheever and his men, and they can't get back at us. There's no way of surrounding us or getting behind. Not a shred of cover anywhere."

"Hope the wind doesn't change," Zera remarked, glancing anxiously at the sky.

"Hot enough as it is," Lee said. He'd peeled off a sweatshirt and tied it around the head and shoulders of the pit bull, trying to protect Melmoth from the cascade of glowing ash that fell silently around them.

"We'll recce up there. Then I cut back here and show myself over the top of the valley head. They come after me. I run and dive in here, and we blow the living shit out of them."

Everybody nodded in silent agreement, and they moved on to the wrecked buildings.

There was a maze of low walls and workshops. Windows and roofs were missing, and everything was in frail condition. Every surface was an inch deep in golden ash and dust. Even as they looked around, they felt a sinister shifting of the earth beneath them, and the mountain opposite seemed to tremble.

"Smoke's coming out at a different angle," said Lee.

"What's that?" asked Kate, pointing at the side of the volcano.

"What?"

"There, halfway up. Oh, it's gone now. I thought I saw some smoke or steam coming out of the slope. This side, not the other."

"Can't make out anything," Dave said. "But it's hard to see properly. Let's all take five."

ROXANNE WAS CRYING, tears coursing through the layers of dirt, turning bright yellow as they dripped. She rode hanging on to Ellie around the waist. Their horse had picked its careful way down into the stinking depths of the narrow valley. Now they were climbing again, toward the ridge.

"Don't cry, Roxie," said her older sister, over her shoulder. "You know it pisses him off."

"But I can't breathe. My throat hurts and I keep on coughing and I want to stop and rest."

"Maybe at the top. We'll be there in a half hour or so. Just hang on and stop crying! Don't let him see you—or else."

A FEW SMALL FLAKES of snow were falling, fluttering along over the orange rocks like specks of white dust. Dave realized with some surprise that winter, old-fashioned winter, would soon be closing in on them. Maybe in a few days. A month at the outside.

But life was going to change in the next thirty minutes or so.

He was lying down, idly rubbing his hand under Melmoth's muzzle, something that the dog had always liked. Lee was sitting opposite Dave, his back against a tumbled wall. Zera lay on her side a few yards farther along, eyes closed.

Idly Dave looked to see where Kate was when it struck him that she was nowhere to be seen.

"Lee?"

"Yeah? Is it time to move, Dad?"

"Soon... Where's Kate gone?"

"She's... Hey, that's double-strange."

Dave Rand felt a sudden stirring of sickness in the pit of his stomach. He was on his feet, and his voice rose in pitch, "What, Lee?"

"Well, she went outside and said she wanted... but that must've been..." He jumped up, waking Zera, who blinked and rubbed at her eyes.

"What's the matter? Is Sheever coming?" She scrambled up, looking around. "Where's Kate gone?"

"I don't know," said Dave, starting to move outside the ruined building. "But I have a fucking good idea and I hope it's wrong."

In his heart, the man knew that his hunch was right. He knew where Kate had gone and what she was doing.

21

Sheever was first over the rise.

He heeled his horse up the last few steep yards, then reined in, tugging so hard that the stallion bucked onto its hind legs, hooves flailing at the stinking air. Fighting it back under his control, the huge man held up a gloved hand to halt the rest of his command.

The woman seemed to have sprung from the dusty earth. She stood about three hundred yards ahead of him, hands on hips. She wore a torn parka that might once have been a pale green, thermal pants and muddy boots. Her face was turned toward him, and the sulfurous wind was blowing at her mane of jet-black hair.

Sheever was almost certain she was one of the group of four that had been trailing him and his men for some time.

He considered dismounting and putting a bullet through her from his rifle, but the swirling smoke and shimmering heat of the erupting volcano made it a risky shot. And there was so much more to be said for having the woman alive.

With the trained eye of a soldier, the big man looked around, standing in the stirrups.

He took in the lay of the land, wondering immediately where the other three were and seeing the group of scattered ruins away to the left. The main trail ahead cut right, along the flank of the volcano, then snaked left, toward the derelict buildings. If there was an ambush, then it would be there.

Sheever's labyrinthine mind calculated all of this. Looking at the woman, he worked out distances and angles. There was yet another track that cut sharp left and would carry them above and beyond the ruins. That option offered the most safety. He could just ride straight on and ignore the woman, whatever she did. Or he could send in a dozen men on the best mounts to pursue her and ride her down. His guess was that she'd got it critically wrong. If she was a decoy, then she'd come a crucial few yards too far.

He turned in the saddle and beckoned for Lemuel to join him.

DAVE BANGED HIS FIST against the crumbling brick wall. "She's gone too far. If he comes at a good gallop, he'll reach her before she can get here!"

The ground vibrated, and bits of the wall shivered under his hand. Dust fell. The snow had ceased, and it was amazingly hot. More pebbles, glowing white-hot, dropped around them, bringing the smell of burning chemicals. It was difficult to be sure, but for a moment he thought he'd seen a trail of light and a steam plume from the nearer side of the turbulent mountain.

But movement from Kate and from the figure on the white horse distracted him.

SHEEVER'S TRAINING with his men bore fruit. It took less than a minute for him and his lieutenant to pick out their best dozen riders.

Kate Mazursky hadn't moved. She watched the developments, wondering if the plan was going to work. For a brief time she'd be running in dead ground, unable to see where Dave Rand, Lee and Zera were waiting for her. That would be the closest to the trembling slopes of the volcano. Above her there was a strange brittle cracking sound, like someone breaking an enormous sheet of mica.

But her eyes were on the blond man on the prancing snow-white stallion.

"Oh!" she gasped, spinning on her heel and starting her sprint for safety. The group of other horsemen seemed to have come from nowhere and were charging at her with an unimaginable speed, halving the gap in a matter of a dozen beats of her panicking heart.

"Go!" breathed Dave, clutching the stock of the Heckler & Koch.

Dust and smoke drifted across the scorched land, making it almost impossible to see what was happening below them.

"Let's go meet her!" shouted Lee.

"Can't."

"Why?"

"If she makes it that far, they'll be on top and they'll chill us all. If she doesn't . . ."

Kate had vanished into the dip, the horsemen already less than four hundred yards behind her, the first of them disappearing into the dead ground. Sheever sat his horse and watched.

Everyone waited.

"On foot, she might not lose too much," said Zera, looking through the hole where a window had long ago rotted away.

"There!" whooped Lee. "She's still going."

Stumbling slightly, weaving from side to side as she fought for breath, Kate Mazursky came over the lip of the rise, her back to the volcano.

The riders weren't yet in sight, and for a handful of precious seconds Dave Rand began to believe that Zera was right and the young woman might make it. His finger crept onto the trigger of the gun.

Then the side of the mountain blew out.

It happened in an erratic slow motion, both quicker than real time and yet infinitely stretched.

Dave's eye was caught by a jagged scar that peeled open in the flank of the volcano, several hundred feet above the trail, close to the vomiting cone. A huge jet of what he knew must be superheated steam gushed out with a deafening whistling sound.

It soared way over their heads, spreading ever wider. Dave ducked, feeling a sensation of intense *damp* heat.

As he looked up again, he gazed into the gaping maw of hell itself. It was as if the mountain were spreading itself obscenely wide, showing a strip of molten rock, dazzling silver-white and gold at its center, merging into veined crimson.

"God save us," Zera screamed at the top of her voice. She was less than six feet away from him, but Dave could hardly catch a whisper of her words.

The lava gushed out in an unstoppable river, faster than a horse could gallop, pouring down the flank of the volcano, straight into the path of the fleeing woman and her pursuers.

Horrified, helpless, Dave watched the rumbling avalanche of death gather momentum as it neared the trail.

On the crest of the ridge, Sheever fought his terrified horse while most of his men dismounted to calm their animals.

"Back down the valley?" Lemuel shouted.

"Have it roasting your ass in ten minutes. No, get 'em organized and we'll take that sharp left trail up higher."

"Sure."

"And bring the girls to me. I want them right at my side."

The heat was so intense that Dave and the others pulled up their hoods to try to protect their faces. The whole land danced and rocked and the air was choking.

But none of them could take their eyes off the tiny figure of Kate Mazursky.

Behind her the first of the dozen horsemen appeared, spurring for their lives. Then, like some primeval monster, the lapping edge of the lava brimmed up at their heels.

The sound of the fresh eruption was so overwhelming that it filled the ears, but even so, the watchers could still hear the screams of the horses as they were swallowed, one by one, into the fiery torment of the molten rock.

The ground rose toward the buildings, and for a moment it seemed there was just a chance that Kate's lead might bear her clear.

Then that moment passed.

"No," whispered Dave. "Oh, Jesus, no."

At the very last second, all hope withered, they saw Kate turn to face her doom. She lifted her arms before her eyes, then vanished in a flare of smoke and heat.

The lava, having consumed its prey, turned itself lazily toward the north, following the contours of lower ground.

If Kate had been able to cover another twenty running strides, she would have been safe.

Lee and Zera were both weeping, their heads buried in their hands. Dave looked down to where the young woman had perished, and he remembered something she'd said—said not so long ago.

"Right at the end, we all go alone."

And his eyes filled with tears of sadness and anger.

EPILOGUE

Sheever and the stunned remnants of his gang walked their horses slowly up the steep trail that would carry them still farther to the west.

They passed within three hundred yards of the group of ruined buildings, but the tall man rode by, head lowered, ignoring it. In his heart he suspected that the other three pursuers were hiding there. But with his men shattered and exhausted, a frontal attack would only lead to more expensive casualties and possibly even to defeat.

"There will be another day, whoever you fuckers are," he said, glancing around to make sure that the chestnut mare with the sisters on its back was close to him. The younger one was still crying softly.

DAVE, LEE AND ZERA watched the imposing figure on horseback from the shadows. Silhouetted against the farther dusty hillside, Sheever was a possible target.

Dave picked up the Sauer rifle and worked the bolt, sliding a round into the chamber then raising it to his shoulder and squinting through the scope sight. His eyes were blurred, and he wiped them clean, lifting the gun a second time, leveling it so that the cross hairs centered on the chest of the snow-headed man. His finger tightened on the trigger. Despite the smoke and fumes, it was worth a shot.

SHEEVER REINED IN the stallion and looked around, beckoning to Ellie Rand. "Here. I'll take her," he said.

He swept Roxanne out of the double saddle with one hand and settled her astride his own mount, folding her to his chest and holding her tight against him. He clicked his tongue to make the horse move on again.

DRAWING a long, slow breath, Dave Rand lowered the rifle, his eyes fixed on Sheever and his daughter.

"Come another day," he said. "Come another day, I swear."

On the savage frontier of tomorrow,
survival is a brand-new game.

SURVIVAL 2000

FROZEN FIRE
James McPhee

David Rand faces his final test—in the third book of Gold Eagle's
SURVIVAL 2000 series.

In the cruel new world created by the devastation of asteroid impacts,
Rand's family is held captive by a murderous gang of army deserters.

With a fortress established in a crumbling mall, the enemy will always
hold the high ground unless Rand can pass the test in a world where
winners die hard . . . and losers live to tell the tale.

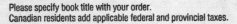

The Executioner's battle against South American drug lords rages on in Book II of The Medellín Trilogy.

DON PENDLETON'S
THE EXECUTIONER

EVIL KINGDOM

The odds of winning are getting slimmer by the minute as the situation heats up. PHOENIX FORCE is trapped in a surprise invasion, one of ABLE TEAM's members is missing, and THE EXECUTIONER is moving in on Colombia's reigning drug czar.

For this powder keg of action, be sure to get your copy of EVIL KINGDOM!

Available in June at your favorite retail outlet, or order your copy now:

THE MEDELLÍN TRILOGY

BOOK I : Blood Rules (THE EXECUTIONER #149)	$3.50 ☐
BOOK II : Evil Kingdom (352-page MACK BOLAN)	$4.50 ☐
BOOK III: Message to Medellin (THE EXECUTIONER #151)	$3.50 ☐
Total Amount	_____
Plus 75¢ postage ($1.00 in Canada)	_____
Total Payable	_____

Please send a check or money order payable to Gold Eagle Books:

In the U.S.
Gold Eagle Books
3010 Walden Ave.
P.O. Box 1325,
Buffalo, NY 14269-1325

In Canada
Gold Eagle Books
P.O. Box 609,
Fort Erie, Ontario
L2A 5X3

Canadian residents add applicable federal and provincial taxes.

Please Print:

Name: _____

Address: _____

City: _____

State/Prov.: _____

Zip/Postal Code: _____

SB23-1